Perpetual Grace

By
Paula Hall

I dedicate this book to my loving husband, David. Through David's guidance and support, I have been able to write about the mosaic of experiences I call "life reflections of grace." He expresses our teamwork: "I do what I do so you can do what you do. Paula, your work is what matters."

David's God-affirming influence in the business arena has a far-reaching impact, and I hope I can support his endeavors as well as he has undergirded mine.

I express my gratitude to God, Creator of Heaven and Earth, and ask Him not to let me waste one moment of daylight.

"We must carry out the works of Him who sent Me as long as it is day; night is coming when no one can work." John 9:4

Introduction

Take a look around, and you will likely see people of all ages showing what they believe in. T-shirts proudly promote

superheroes, ball caps shout logos of sports teams, bumper stickers tell what political candidates we like, and bracelets call out our connection to charitable causes. I myself love graphic T-shirts. I often wear ones with "Love" printed on them or Snoopy painting Easter eggs. One special shirt has "Kindness is Free" inscribed. I like to wear it when I travel. People in the airport respond with kindness when they read the phrase across my chest.

My favorite T-shirt is my "Grace" shirt. Not "Amazing Grace", not "Saved by Grace," not "Grace-lest anyone should boast," or not even "Grace Changes Everything"—Just "Grace."

It is THE one word that helps me begin…and it is the reason I write this tome.

I found a calm refuge in God by His Grace. After a few years of pondering, scribbling, jotting, noting, discussing, and writing, restlessness left my pen, and I considered words necessary to be issued for my children-that is adult "children". So I got on with it.

Grace. Beautiful Grace.

Grace to many is simple elegance. Observant Christians sing robustly for seven verses declaring life-changing attributes of Amazing Grace.

Grace is God's gift of unfailing love, mercy, strength, refuge, steadfastness, sovereignty, and forgiveness freely offered to me--well, everyone. The Favor of God inspired John Newton to compose his most recognizable hymn. The Favor of God is Jesus Christ, Savior of the Universe, sacrificed for me, the offender by God's mighty plan. God Incarnate.

Grace is what sets God, Christianity, apart from all other religions. Hindus have karma, Buddhists have the Eightfold plan, Jews have the Moses covenant, Muslims have the Law of Allah– and in all these religions, there is something that must be attained--a work to be done. God, through His Son Jesus, has given us Grace.

The essence of my faith is "the conviction of things not seen," however, there are opportunities for my senses to experience God, and these vignettes I recorded are insights based through the lens of grace. Having a Methodist influence infused in my bones, I utilized John Wesley's naming of graces to arrange my thoughts:

Prevenient Grace: the grace that goes before

Justifying Grace: the grace of forgiveness when turning toward God

Sanctifying Grace: the grace of God's presence to restore the holiness of the heart

I have not visually seen God-- more on that later-- but I know that He has been more than one-dimensional in my life.

My thoughts on earthly life and eternity were sowed early, beginning at home and Tyson Methodist Church. I feel an urgency at this stage in my life to name the human expressions and vivid signs of Life in the Spirit. I believe that there is nothing foreign to the Spirit that the Spirit embraces all. Even our mundane experiences contain all the stuff of holiness and of human growth in grace. Much of it goes unnoticed. We fail so often to recognize the light that shines through the windows and dusty panes of our daily lives. We are too busy to name the events that bless the ordinary, holy in its uniqueness, but I want to tell you there are many burning bushes–and we must have hearts that allow our eyes to see them.

The everydayness of my recollections is none above anyone else since ever. But they are mine. Do my writings matter? Did Etheria, Eudocia, and Augustine of Hippo perceive a call to register their accounts and thoughts on their God-filled life, or was it ***given*** in the outflow of their being? I ponder this…

These accounts are reflections of the grace that has been poured over me. Poured like a gentle fountain at times and like cascading falls when I needed it most — when I was totally unaware and when discipleship was costly.

It is grace that allows us to excel in our assignments and business on earth. It is grace, not knowledge or association, that makes saints.

I am walking, stumbling, running with grace in this life into eternity, where I pray it will be swallowed up in glory.

Paula M. Hall

FOREWORD

My mom has a special gift. Our family moved from central Indiana to Wisconsin when I was a young child. Since then, my mom has always been able to spot when someone else is from Indiana. Whether it be on a family vacation or at the grocery store, she would introduce herself and share that she was from Frankfort, Indiana. I knew I inherited that gift from my mom when I met Paula, because I could tell right away that she was a girl from Indiana. And when I visited Paula's house for the first time, I knew from her beautiful antique furnishings – they looked just like my grandmother's. Of course, I told her I was born in Frankfort.

The personal and charming stories shared in *Perpetual Grace* drew me in so tight, it made me feel like I was right there with her in Versailles. These accounts of her life touched my heart, reminding me so much of the stories I heard about my mom and dad growing up in Frankfort. I have such a fondness of the town where I was born as we visited my grandparents and other family there regularly. Small town Indiana is a very special place and full of grace. It was meaningful to experience Paula's childhood and young adult years through this book. And no matter where you are from, you will find joy in these timeless examples of grace through ordinary circumstances.

I met Paula for the first time, more than 25 years ago, when she was leading Deborah Circle, a women's group at our church in St. Charles. That day when I nervously showed up for the first time, she read and taught from chapter 11 of the Book of Hebrews. But she didn't just read it, she recited it with authority! Though I was raised in a Methodist church like Paula, I was not a Bible scholar like she appeared to be. But as she began to teach on the reading, I was immediately put at ease as she shared with so much grace. She pulled me into the examples of faith recorded in that chapter and inspired me to want to know more. Never did she put anyone down for not knowing something, but instead she invited us to learn and grow *with* her.

I continued to study scripture and learn from Paula in the Bible study group she led called Deborah by the Palm, which you will read about in this book. It was in this group, and other classes at our church, that I started to understand about the different "graces". Accepting the gift of grace was a big step as a young believer, but then I learned there are different types of grace with very confusing, long names. How could I ever keep track? Paula's writing in *Perpetual Grace* gives beautiful examples of the teachings of John Wesley and Prevenient, Justifying, and Sanctifying Grace. Through these illustrations, we can learn and experience the beauty of the precious gifts that God has given us through his son, Jesus.

The pages of *Perpetual Grace* provide a cohesive storyline interweaving Paula's rich history of the people God carefully placed in her life. These people became the vessels that shaped her into the Christ-follower she is today. Her stories incorporate beautifully written context, scripture, witness, and application. If you are a believer, this book will inspire you to consider your own grace story. I cannot help but think about the people who God placed in my life and how His grace has molded me. I consider the art, music, liturgy, and other things that I possibly took for granted or that went unnoticed, but now realize their importance in my spiritual growth. This book sparks ideas in my own mind about how I can share about God's grace in my life to others. And if you are not a believer, this book could very well be a teaching of the Prevenient Grace already present in your life and a nudge from the Holy Spirit to consider the Justifying and Sanctifying Grace being offered to you by Jesus Christ.

It is an honor and joy to write this Foreword to *Perpetual Grace*. Paula has been and always will be my teacher and my friend. I am so thankful and give Glory to God that He is using my sister in Christ to disciple me and others by sharing her encounters of grace.

All this is for your benefit, so that the grace that is reaching more and more people
may cause thanksgiving to overflow to the glory of God. 2 Corinthians 4:15

Foreword by Jennifer Swenson

Prevenient Grace
The Unmerited Assistance That Comes Before

Prevenient grace "precedes human action and **reflects God's heart for his creation**. *It testifies to* **God's being the initiator of any relationship** *with him and reveals him as* **one who pursues us**."—*Andrew Dragos*

The Grace of Unconditional Love

Indiana
1965

"You're blessed when you're content with just who you are—no more, no less."
- Matthew 5:5, _The Message_

"...I like you just the way you are." — Fred Rogers

"There's my perfect child," Grandma Pete exclaimed as she climbed out of the car, high heels clicking on the concrete sidewalk as she walked toward our house. "Ready to go?"
"I'll be right there! I'll get my suitcase. Did you buy the green grapes?" I asked in eager excitement.
"Yes, we will have them when we get home," she assured me.
From the front porch, I scrambled into the kitchen to retrieve my navy-red-green swirly-colored kiddy suitcase. Grandma Pete was known as "Evelyn" to her work colleagues in Indianapolis. Her nickname "Pete" was from
her maiden name "Peters" and it had stuck all through the years. My maternal grandfather, Harland, died before I was two. After her workweek as a state supreme court secretary, she traveled back to the farm in southern Indiana and picked me up on Friday afternoons. I thought this weekend getaway was solely for my benefit; it never occurred to me that my parents were glad to have a

night's reprieve.

After I climbed in her car, we drove through the State Park and arrived at Grandma's four-square farmhouse in about fifteen minutes. At the end of a gravel dead-end road, the white house stood tall against the fields and wooded ravines. Wildlife roamed in the woods that formed the backdrop to my grandma's farm. Deer, wild turkey, and pheasants lurked in the shadows. Pesky possums and raccoons were frequent passersby.

The house was basic, with no heat on the second floor. It had a staircase that scares my husband today–steep, narrow, and not quite the right angle. Until the middle 70s, Grandma used a corded phone with a party line. These arrangements suited Grandma just fine, even though she was using the best technology at work. Yes, the house was basic-basic. But to me, this was a royal retreat.

Very content, Grandma and I spent Friday evening together. "We" often baked pies. She would put a crust in a small aluminum pan with cinnamon and sugar for me. We cut out Betsy McCall's paper dolls or took a walk down the

gravel lane, clickety-clacking our "thongs" (as we called our matching flip-flops). I would lay on the moss-green area rug reading a book while Grandma puttered around.

When I tracked dust into the house, not a word was said. Before bedtime, we had Black Cows, the most delicious ice cream treat with vanilla scoops piled high and Coca-Cola poured over. The Coke would be chilled, so it would form small crystals atop the ice cream.

At night, I crawled into Grandma Pete's double bed, where I sometimes slept. The room was very small, and there was a window to the east about two feet from the bed. One night, when I was about three, I got into bed.

"You can't sleep on that side of the bed. There is a GIRAFFE on that side," Grandma Pete commented.

Well, OK–I am not going to sleep on that side if there is a giraffe–you can have it, Grandma," I thought.

A while later, I explained that I was scared of the giraffe on the window side of the bed.

Grandma laughed and hugged me, "No honey, a DRAFT comes in from the window…"

Saturday mornings at the castle were a delight.

With one hand on her hip, Grandma would take my order for breakfast.

Every time: "What would you like for breakfast?"

Every answer: "I'll have sausage and hot chocolate."

Request and reply were made in a royal tone. The order had been expected and respected. The dialogue crisp and direct.

The order was elegantly served on a Johnson Brothers Blue Willow plate–a small salad plate. Two iron-skillet-fried sausage patties were placed in front of me on the table as I gazed westward out the window. The hot chocolate was also in blue willow cup and saucer. This was befitting the imperial morning. I sometimes stayed another night, and Mom would pick me up on Sunday morning. Saturday nights, the theme songs of Mary Tyler Moore, Bob Newhart, and Carol Burnett became the backdrop to catching lightning bugs, making homemade ice cream, and reading books on the front porch in Adirondack chairs.

Carol Burnett would sing me to bed, "I was so glad we had this time together…"

Little did she know how glad I was…

Until Grandma died at 95 years old, in June of 2013, on the "longest" day of the year, she would always greet me, "Hello, how is my *perfect child*…?" A blessed assurance in a fractured world. The evening before her funeral, there was a brilliant rainbow above her home. The foursquare farmhouse… that I am now renovating so my family will not miss out on the blessings the farm has to offer.

Grandma's unconditional love communicated the beauty of being accepted. This is the essence of prevenient grace. I was loved for who I was without having to work for it. In All my dirt tracking, clickety-clacking, sausage, and hot-chocolate neediness, my presence was always welcomed. Grandma and I enjoyed beautiful moments of togetherness.

Being with God, you experience beautiful moments and enjoy being together. We must stop trying to make ourselves lovable to God and simply receive His great love while recognizing that we are unworthy of it. He sent his Son to make us "perfect…"

I was born into and under grace.
God reigns. Grace reigns…
And sometimes it just rains…I am thankful God has given me the strength to endure the storms.

The Grace of Memories

Indiana
1930s-present

Grandma Pete lived in the same house on a farm for seventy-two years. Grandpa Harland's mother and father bought it shortly before the war, and it became the newlyweds' home. In the 1930s, the home did not have running water, and the road stopped about 200 yards from the dwelling. When a well was dug and an outhouse installed, the couple had a country home to live in. Now my mom lives there. Like the English TV home show on the Dabl network, it is "Escape to the Country." And like a fleeing Londoner, she has a countryside retreat with historical value, serene views, and a sanctuary for wildlife as well as mortals. Returning to this beloved white farmhouse down the long gravel dead-end road is familiar. The road ***does*** come all the way back to the house today. The two-story, four-square house in southeastern Indiana is protected from the outside world. Bittersweet vines hang from the trees, and blackberries grow against the fence in a narrow strip clinging to the barbed wire in a row. The straight line makes it easy to pick the fruit when it ripens. Wild turkeys, deer, and occasional skunk families run through the yard. A picturesque fog rises in the morning from the ravine.

There is a light switch in the kitchen that has remained unchanged for all these years; the switch plate is a chef. A Yellow Waving Chef. I call him "Mr. Yellow Chef." Mr. Chef has one arm up, waving. When flipped on, it makes a loud "click." Sometime over the years, the flip switch was replaced with a round dimmer that sticks out over the Chef's belly. The round knob must be firmly pressed for light to appear– and the click is intact.

The click creates an aromatherapy for my soul. The sound releases memories that ease my anxiety, reduce stress, and alleviate the discomfort of the burdens of the world. The therapeutics associated with Mr. Yellow Chef tumbles into my head, releasing smells and comfort without a single pan on the stove or delight in the oven.

9

Mr. Chef has one arm up, waving. When flipped on, it makes a loud "click."

Sometime over the years, the flip switch was replaced with a round dimmer that sticks out over the Chef's belly. The round knob must be firmly pressed for light to appear– and the click is intact.

The click is aromatherapy for my soul! The sound releases memories that ease my anxiety, reduce stress, and alleviate the discomfort of the burdens of the world. The therapeutics associated with Mr. Yellow Chef tumble into my head, releasing smells and comfort without a single pan on the stove or delight in the oven.

"O tidings of comfort and joy, comfort and joy,
O tidings of comfort and joy..."
-Refrain from God Rest Ye Merry Gentlemen, Old English Song

The Grace of Knowing

For goodness sake, you don't fall in love with a guy watching Monday night football with his friends just because he agrees to give you a ride home from college.

But I did.

David and I met at Butler University when I was a freshman and he was a senior. Stephanie, my forever friend, had worked with him during the summer and told me he was "nice" and I should look him up. I don't know if it was her prompt or if it was the Holy Spirit, but in the first month of being at school I said hello in the cafeteria and I wandered over to the men's dorm on Monday evening (yes, there was such a thing back in the day) and asked for a ride home even though I had a vehicle at school to drive myself. So…I believe it may have been some heavenly help on the inclination to ask him.

All the tangible things I remember do not add up to "why I fell in love."
This is why we love one another:
The Counsel of the Wise and Great observed from heaven and planted our paths together to "have and to hold and be united as one."
It is an elaborate explanation, but it is the only one I can allow. Too many remarkable coincidences occur in sequence, and obstacles are removed to otherwise permit our relationship. With confidence, I say this "explanation" can be used by *anyone* if they acknowledge Who is writing the script."

Our story parallels many others. Young love. Romance. I thought he was the best. I would use every superlative to describe David. *Best* at everything. I fell for him in a great way.
Dated. Engagement. Wedding. We work. We have children. We do life as it comes. Faithful love. Many anniversaries.

Marriage is at root not about feelings, which come and go, ask anyone who has been married for any length of time, but about keeping a promise. You promise to love one another "for better, for worse…until death do you part" in front of family and friends and God.

I still use superlatives when describing David. Best-the best husband for me. He is the Most Humble man (since Moses). He is the Kindest person I know. He is the Most Resilient person in the family.

My feelings have grown deeper for him since the day I made the promises. We complete each other's thoughts and we know submitting to one another is an avenue to joy that only we can share. It is life-giving when both are in constant care for each other. We are not perfect: Feelings of exasperation still come–however, the promise stands.

Did the football angels have David sitting in his dorm room with friends on that Monday night, September 15, 1980? David, the avid Browns fan, would have been watching no matter what. The Browns played the Oilers and lost the game, but won the division title. The Brown's nickname that year was "The Kardiac Kids." Their fourth-quarter scoring frenzies gave people heart palpitations. The game they lost that September night gave *my heart* someone to love forever and many heart flutters. They truly were "The Kardiac Kids."

The Grace of Home

Versailles, Indiana
1960s

Isaiah 32:18: "My people will live in peaceful dwelling places, in secure homes, in undisturbed places of rest."

In my childhood home, I was surrounded by rural rhythms, which were a form of security. A hundred yards from our house, we had a grain elevator for our grain operation. There were round silver metal bins, a leg that took the grain to the three bins, a dryer, and a large pole building to house all the farmy-farm stuff. There were three older buildings alongside the granary. At night during harvest, I would fall asleep to the sound of sifting grain going back and forth from the bins to the dryer and the dryer igniting to process the material. The sifting was interrupted by blowing and hydraulic shuffles.

Dust particles danced in the pole light rays. This was my Joffrey Ballet and New York Philharmonic. Each movement of the harvest was an arrangement differing by the weight, moisture, and composition of the day's reaping. The combine would lumber in with the tractor trailing behind, pulling the gravity bed. The crash of the metal wagon, filled to the top, hitting a large pothole in the barn lot, sounded like a kettle drum. The sound of grinding gears, the smell of grain, and the headlights swerving through my screened window were a country lullaby.

God's provision of grace not only came through the ample harvest but also through the soothing comfort of home.

The living room was where the polished cotton sofa would remain cool in the summer, and the upright Wurlitzer piano stood in the east picture window light. The walls heard hundreds and hundreds of hours of practicing and playing on the black and white keys with not one rebuke of missed notes or improper tempo. This room was warm and inviting; it faced the kitchen where mom cooked. The refrigerator was always stocked full, and the adjoining laundry room had a freezer with Schwann ice cream ready for dipping. Mom always provided stability and direction. Form follows function. Mom and Frank Lloyd Wright knew that the spiritual union of form and function was imperative. Be humble, be strong, climb the mountain today gives you; kindness counts, and say thank you while climbing—wherever it takes you.

I don't take for granted the love given when I was growing up to where I was going. My being formed in quiet obscurity. Our small life matters. Function followed from this grounded life. Obscurity, perhaps, is of infinite worth? Jesus lived a simple, hidden life in a small town. A carpenter that built "things" and then eternity for humanity. Form followed function from his home. My beloved Reverend Tom Walker meditated on the value of home:

"Deep inside of me, in a place I can't seem to define or touch, there is a longing for something called home. It is more than a nostalgia for the simpler days of growing up. It is rooted in being itself. It is tied to a question: Why am I here?... So, the journey begins with a longing for home. This is one of the continuous threads in everyone's life journey. Something in each of us longs for home.

"In his book, *The Longing for Home*, Frederick Buechner writes: 'Home summons up a place...a place where you feel you belong and which in some sense belongs to you, a place where you feel that all is somehow ultimately well even if things aren't going well at any given moment.'"

Walker continues: "Home is where it is safe. It is where we feel secure and protected from the outside world. As I grow older, I have sensed myself wanting to hold on, wanting to capture and savor each moment and not let go. I experience it early on a summer morning, sitting on our patio, listening to the birds. I can push the world back and hear the invitation of Jesus to come and receive his promise of rest.

"I know the ache of loneliness. It goes deeper than not having a congregation to serve anymore. It is the loneliness of simply being human, of yearning for something I can't find. I can be with people and have satisfying conversations. I can enjoy summer evening walks with Ellyn or time with friends, but that loneliness always returns. What is it?

"Can it be that home, at least the home we seek, is not just a place of people or a safe space, but something else? The ache of longing is recorded in many of the Psalms. In Psalm 42, the writer expresses his longing as a great deep thirst for God: 'As a deer longs for flowing streams, So my soul longs for you, O God. My soul thirsts for God, For the living God....'"

As Tom so aptly expressed, our deepest longing is for the *home* that we find in God alone. My childhood home is another way God showered his prevenient grace in my life, preparing me to come to know Him as my one true home.

Psalm 91:1-2 "Whoever dwells in the shelter of the Most High will rest in the shadow of the Almighty. I will say of the LORD, 'He is my refuge and my fortress, my God, in whom I trust.'"

The Grace of Beauty

Indianapolis, Indiana
1960s

In the 1960s, my dad had a boss who lived in Indianapolis. When I first set foot in the boss' home, I thought I had entered an elegant show home that only the rich could afford. It was a large ranch with a courtyard.

The house had a beautiful fireplace—beautiful in a transcendent way. More than being homey and saying, "Sit down and stay awhile," the home spoke: "Your presence is welcomed here." The rich-toned brick fireplace stretched across the front of the living room with a soft-corduroy type earth colored furniture surrounding the opening. Or was it leather? The memory of the place is comfort: It was to be tumbled into by the family at the end of a long day with a radiant, warm fire burning, and laughter would come easily and conversations flowing long into the night. This was my first thought as I walked into the home.

The couple had a son about my age (annoying Alan Drane), but he had this stuffed animal: a lion. Not any lion, but one that had a cord to pull. When pulled, the lion roared or said something in a gruff voice. It was love at first sight. The lion reminded me of Aslan, the great lion, representing God's love and beauty in C. S. Lewis's Narnia.

13

We walked into the living room. A built-in bookshelf ran across one wall filled with books and things that were beautiful. Small glass figurines, historical family pictures, a vase with flowers, and trinkets that were silver, gold and attractive to the eye. The light filtered into the room from the courtyard. Maybe I imagined it–were these items from faraway places?

Inside that home, I gained a thirst for beauty that has never left me. In front of the lovely fireplace, the lion was shown to me-- or it "spoke" to me. Funny how He appears in unusual places... a burning bush, a pillar of cloud or fire, or in front of a suburban Midwest fireplace in a ranch home.

 The word "beauty" does not often occur in the Bible, but the celebration of the loveliness of creation occurs throughout the Bible. Israel was built with artistic designers. The artists were enabled by the Holy Spirit to create amazing things to honor God. Bezalel and Oholiab hammered two golden cherubims into the cover of the ark of the covenant in the desert. God revealed beauty to these artists.

After the instructions for the place of worship were given, God inscribed the law on stone with his finger and handed it to Moses. Beauty was personal to him. The finger of God, an anthropomorphism, is used four times in Scripture, and each time, it indicates his power and majesty. A stone tablet was given to Moses with commands—instructions in God's handwriting. The mighty creator of the universe "wrote" Israel's guidebook. He didn't give them an impersonal message. It is the difference between cards I have from my great-grandmother signed in her cramped arthritic fingers, giving her small, curving, cursive a shaken look, but the message was strong, —"Lots of Love, Grandma Burton" versus an email sent from someone with the perfect black New Times Roman typed word, "Love."

There is beauty in the signature of God. In the signature of mortals.

What is more beautiful than the majesty of God?

 In my homes, I have created a "Corner Beautiful"—a bookshelf across one wall filled with books and my beautiful things, just like the bookshelf in the home of my father's boss so long ago. Thank you, Alan Drane, for being annoying and showing me your lion. Aslan would be delighted.

The Grace of a Shepherd

1960s-1970s

John 10:14-15 Jesus said, "I am the good shepherd; I know my sheep and my sheep know me—just as the Father knows me and I know the Father—and I lay down my life for the sheep."

One Sunday, as I listened to the sermon in my childhood church, I felt like I was being lulled to sleep. Soft droning from the pulpit blended with morning sunlight through the prismed glass to create a deep anesthetic. The Pastor's voice was like that of Charlie Brown's parents–no words were audible, only a soft noise. No arrow of meaning was penetrating my heart. I was insensitive to any outside stimulation, until–I heard my father's name–I mean *my* dad. I was fully alert! The minister spoke of Jesus the Good Shepherd, who said, "My sheep listen to my voice, they listen, and they follow me." The minister explained that as he drove home one day, he saw that our cattle had escaped through a hole in the fence. The neighbor had tried to rustle them back into the field with no luck. The cowboy-rustling minister gave it a whirl, yelling and hee-hawing, "Over here, over here, come back, cows, come back!"

The neighbors phoned Dad, who scurried across the way. Dad *called out* to the cattle, and they came to him. The cows recognized their owner's voice.

"They hear my voice…" (John 10:27) expresses personal intimacy. When someone knows Jesus well, they recognize the one who feeds them or cares for them and the one they trust. The minister expounded on how we *hear* God's voice and grow intimate with Christ. Humanity is fitly compared to sheep in this parable of Jesus. They are called sheep of his pasture. Ugh. I think I had strayed from the pasture during the sermon…

The sheepfold represents a place of security, a protective shelter of the family of God. No one can enter the fold except through the Good Shepherd—Jesus. He alone determines who can come in. Hearing my dad's name from the pulpit was a little startling to me. I am not thinking of Jesus at this point. I am thinking perhaps he will be calling my name next. In a panic that lasted a fraction of a second, **I worried that the Pastor was listing those who did not attend church often.**

Nope.

He used my dad's calling of cattle to illustrate the voice of Jesus.

Dad, who did not attend church except on the high holidays–Christmas, Easter, and when I played a solo—made it into the sermon.

An arrow hit me that day.

Grace is unmerited.

Out of his fullness we have all received grace in place of grace already given. - John 1:16

"My sheep listen to my voice; I know them, and they follow me. I give them eternal life, and they shall never perish; no one will snatch them out of my hand. My Father, who has given them to me, is greater than all; no one can snatch them out of my Father's hand. I and the Father are one." - John 10:27-29

The Grace of Waiting

†

We spend a lot of our time waiting. For a bus, for a doctor's appointment, for test results, for the water to boil. Why do I trust it is worth the wait? Waiting is hoping, enduring, and anticipating. Waiting requires faith, patience, humility, and a sense of eternity. The Hebrew word for wait is "kavah." It is an active verb often translated as "to eagerly look for" and is rooted in the concept of twisting/stretching and related to the word "cord" and phrase "bind together." In our waiting, God actively binds us together. People of faith wait in expectation. "Wait for the Lord; be strong and take heart and wait for the Lord." Psalm 27:14

Waiting. Christians wait for the return of the Messiah. Jews are waiting for the Messiah.

How am I to wait?
Why should I wait?
How long must I wait?

"It's your turn to watch for the bus!" Mother's call wafted through the L-shaped ranch farm home.

The house overlooked forty acres of farm fields knitted together in a lovely green and golden pattern. Peering over them, I could see a yellow school bus trekking to the next stop. It could be seen over a mile away, rolling down 50 South past the Adams' place in the morning mist, looking like a toy being pushed by an invisible hand.

Mom wanted us to be waiting roadside when Bus 16 pulled up. When it made a left turn onto our road, out the door, I ran, my sister tagging along behind.

I learned the grace of waiting at a young age. Lamentations 3:25-28 says explicitly that it is good to learn to wait while you are young:

> *"The Lord is good to those whose hope is in him,*
> *to the one who seeks him;*
> *It is good to wait quietly*
> *For the salvation of the Lord.*
> *It is good for a man to bear the yoke*
> *while he is young.*
> *Let him sit alone in silence,*
> *for the Lord has laid it on him."*

Mr. Knigga (Ki-NAY-Gee) was waiting for us, too. He drove the yellow Carpenter bus with great care. The rough-hewn farmer driver wore denim overalls and lived about two miles down the road from us. I don't remember him ever missing a day. (Mr. Walsh was my first bus driver– he had lost a portion of an arm in the D-day invasion in 1944 in Normandy. He was kind and soft-spoken. Mr. and Mrs. Walsh lived a few fields west of our home. I didn't think it was unusual that a man driving my school bus did not have "all" of his arm and only one hand. He was just "Mr. Walsh." He retired, and then Mr. Knigga took over.)

Up the two steps, I would go every morning, scanning the crowded bus. The odd lot, me included, jumbled together each morning with little bother. Allison Dent was always in the front seat, the Cliff kids scattered throughout, Cumberworths in the middle, the trusty Black duo somewhere in the mix, and Wayne Evans and the King boys in the back. I might pick an empty seat if available or sit with any of my fellow riders. We were amicable riders. However, I wouldn't sit in the back. The boys there could be rowdy.

Bus 16 was ecumenical. Everyone rode together without staging protests as they might today. Big kids, little kids, poor and kinda poor were all together. Bullying was based on kids being kids. Sometimes, there were unkind things said, but it rolled off—there was not an attitude of victimhood. Or, if it was too harsh, there was someone who would halt the harassment. The older boys stayed in the back while the younger ones were in front so Mr. Knigga could see what occurred. There were a lot of reasons for scorning, but the bus culture looked out for one another.

The heater would be roaring in the winter and warm my feet. Temperature regulation was pressing in on the tabs on the windows, pulling down a bit and cracking the windows open. Entertainment on the bus was an AM/FM radio. The most requested was WKRQ-FM, Cincinnati, a top 40 hits station. Submitting to the passengers' pleas, Mr. Knigga reached up to dial a knob about head level with his left hand and tuned into the music. With his right hand, he would shift gears and manage the blinking "stop" sign attached to the bus. His eyes peered into the rearview bus mirror that showed the rows of passengers behind him.

During the morning ride there were low murmurs and the early sun fogging up the windows, allowing the passengers to express themselves in finger-doodle art. Peace signs, smiley faces, the year we'd graduate, flowers, arrows, and variations of modern art graced the steamed-up morning windows. One hand swipe from your seatmate would erase your illustration and claim to fame. A few more stops in the country and then into town. The youngest students exited the bus first at the elementary school. Then Mr. Knigga would roll out of the parking lot at the elementary school and drive through town toward my school. Again, we waited; we were dropped off last.
The mood changed after the youngsters were dropped off. Teens sensed the energy that awaited at South Ripley Junior- Senior High. Team Bus 16 knew the last few miles were a preview for the day ahead. We turned right onto Benham Road with a little less than a mile to go.

Book bags jostling, coats adjusting, and noise level rising, we were all ready to disembark. We passed by Ohio Rod Products, the manufacturing complex nestled next to the school. I did not know that this factory held my future father-in-law.

The school day started with a trip to my locker (look for any notes on my locker – the way we communicated) and a quick walk around the building with friends while teachers nodded their heads. I would look for Jerilyn, Kathy, Mindy, Stephanie, Julie, and whoever else might be around, and we would connect. Remember, no cell phones. No texting. It is a face-to-face world. Room 6 —peek in. Anybody working on the paper? The daily gaggle proceeded.

When we started driving to school, it helped our social time. It allowed an earlier arrival, and there was time to walk and talk—more gathering at the lockers and sometimes we would go to the music room to hang out. The bell rang.

After school, Mr. Knigga sat patiently in front of the school as his passengers trickled onto the bus. The heat of the afternoon didn't seem to bother him. His baseball-style cap was a little of-square sometimes, and the high-pitched tenor voice would squeak out "heeello" with a wave. If you were in the front rows, he would strike up a gentle conversation over daily events. A laugh came from his girth if someone told him a joke. Often, he was the joker. Waiting didn't bother Mr. Knigga.

Watching and Waiting.
Even as we wait, God is Watching.
Even as we watch, He is Waiting.

Psalm 121:8 – "The Lord will watch over your coming and going both now and
forevermore."

Some things are worth waiting for....

The King's Grace

1975
"And the master saw that the LORD was with him and that the LORD made all that he did
prosper in his hand. And Joseph found grace in his sight, and he served him..." Genesis 39:
3,4a

I remember Mrs. Green, my third-grade teacher, who was also a family friend. Mrs. Green was the
grandmother of my friend, Stephanie (our moms were friends), and she was friends with my
grandmother as well. Stephanie and I have been friends since birth.
Mrs. Green's classroom was in the basement of the school building. After lunch, when we returned
to her room, she often read aloud from books like *Ramona the Pest*. Her room felt relaxed during
reading in the cool lower-level classroom after our meal and recess.

Mrs. Green was a robust, gray-haired woman who was a favorite with everyone—except, perhaps,
the boys who were "slackers." I recall Billy having to stand in the trash can as punishment—maybe
he wasn't paying attention or was being noisy. Of course, today, a teacher would be reprimanded for
punishing a student this way, but in those days, teachers did not have extra help in the classroom, so
they did what they could to guide the naughty students while teaching the rest of us. The trash can
was better than sending Billy to Mr. Susnick.

Mr. Susnick, the principal.
God save the King.
He was our stately leader. The Imperial King of his tutelage domain.

19

The King's office was on the second floor. When I stepped into the secretarial office, I could see His Majesty's behemoth desk to the left through the door. Nervously, I would glance over to see if the tall, mustached monarch was sitting in the throne room. Sometimes, he would look towards me with his dark brush-like eyebrow lifted. I would look down very quickly and mutter to the secretary whatever I came to the office to retrieve. The King would nod if he caught my eye. His demeanor was reserved—very stately. I cannot remember him ever saying an unkind word to me.

Mr. Susnick carried a meter stick everywhere. Oh Lord, have mercy on me if he ever used it. The measuring stick was his version of a cane. As he walked, it was a gentle guide. But in the minds of all students, it was a weapon of mass destruction. The stick was like a secret weapon he harbored, although it was in plain sight. Every good King has a military force, but Mr. Susnick only needed that stick.

In a country school, the principal was responsible for many duties. He would occasionally come out at recess and stand with the teachers. His presence with that stick was like the National Guard coming into a town to preserve calm during a time of chaos. No girl or boy would dare jump from a swing or shout a curse word with the King in sight.

When the bell rang, everyone lined up quickly with him as the playground monitor and then marched back to class with an obedient spirit. There was no running, pushing, or slipshod activity, with his shadow looming. In his absence, the stairs would sometimes become cluttered, with boys getting in the last jab or girls tagging one another as we climbed our way into the building.

In 5th or 6th grade, there was no teacher at the lunch tables as there were in the lower grades. My friends and I were chatting it up, enjoying the delights of Versailles Elementary's savory selections, when Mr. Susnick slipped into the cafeteria silently. The midday eatery was like most restaurants when people were having a nice time: noisy and boisterous, with voices echoing off the walls. He stood at the head of one of the tables. He must have thought that our volume was not befitting the elementary cafe. Probably one hundred or so kids were in the room, sitting at the long tables, savoring their lunches. Happy serfs in Mr. Susnick's serfdom.

He took the meter stick and slammed it on one of the tables. In his deep voice, he gently said, "You are too loud. Hold it down," and walked away.

One Hundred Dead Children.
The King reigns.

There is a king that reigns in every season of life. A principal, a professor, a landlord, a mortgage, a boss, a sports schedule –even leisure, and we **submit or rebuke its** authority. The choice must be made.

Mr. Susnick was a good king.

"The king said to Daniel, 'Surely your God is the God of gods and the Lord of kings and a revealer of mysteries, for you were able to reveal this mystery.'" - Daniel 2:47 NIV

"But the LORD is the true God; he is the living God, the eternal King. When he is angry, the earth trembles; the nations cannot endure his wrath." - Jeremiah 10:10 NIV

"Then a new king began to rule Egypt, who did not know who Joseph was…" Exodus 1:8

The Grace of Contentment

1970s

"Godliness with contentment is great gain… If we have food and clothing, we will be content with that." - 1 Timothy 6:6, 8 NIV

The basement cafeteria at school was small and orderly. Mrs. Curran, the king's head chef, ran a tight ship. The swinging screen door entry was efficient, letting the hungry children in one by one. The tables were assigned by grade. If you were in lower grades, your teacher would often sit with you. Good manners were encouraged. You waited for your classmates to complete their meals, and everyone left together.

Mom would *not* pack my lunch. Ugh. Instead, I ate hot dogs, hamburgers, grilled cheese, canned peaches, white bread, canned corn, and tater tots, all cooked cafeteria style—and what if you didn't "feel" like a hot dog on Tuesday? Her mantra: "Eat what is served." I was envious of my friends who brought their food in lunch boxes. Cute lunch boxes with pink flowers and Scooby Doo with matching thermoses. Their sandwiches were wrapped in cellophane, and they had a side of cookies and carrot sticks. Boxes inside of boxes. Why did I have to suffer through mediocre food? The most daring move on my part in the cafeteria was choosing chocolate milk. The long-term effect of this grade school cafeteria offense set me up for a lifetime of being able to eat at almost any establishment *without* complaint. It also gave me the ability to create conversation to divert attention away from the culinary selection and be satisfied with the outcome if the food is wonderful–a bonus. If it is cafeteria grade–smile, and do not share your opinion because no one cares that you are a food elitist. Lesson: Culinary anguish improves endurance and creativity.

Hebrews 13:5 - "Keep your lives free from the love of money and be content with what you have, because God has said, 'Never will I leave you; never will I forsake you.'" NIV

Mrs. Curran, the school lunch lady, seemed to always be at the church too. How could she be at the church *and* be preparing our meals at school, too? God had supernaturally given her powers to be the elementary school chef, church custodian, *and* Sunday school teacher. Amazing. One of the first miracles I witnessed.

Mrs. Curran taught Sunday School in a room, or rather a space of approximately eight by ten feet. A child-sized table was allotted to the rectangle with tiny wooden chairs. Mrs. Curran would have to side-squeeze along the wall to gather supplies along the back. There was an accordion door to pull for privacy. She was a welcoming face as I tumbled into the church. Mrs. Curran would nod and give a kind word. She reminded me of Jesus. Mrs. Curran was humble and kind. Like Jesus, she did not draw attention to herself and showed love to the children in Sunday school and elementary school alike. No barriers. If I had been the Samaritan woman at the well, she would have taught me and fed me.

She fed us spiritually, just as she fed us physically. We learned in simple ways. Through a flannel graph story and weekly take-home flyers that had a sheet to color in Jesus. In the tiny space of the church, we learned to be content with what we had. I loved it when we had new crayons. There was a deep continuity between home, church, and school and the physical, spiritual, and emotional nourishment we received in our small community. Everywhere I went, I was being fed. Wonder bread and the Bread of Life were working together.

John 6:35: "Then Jesus declared, 'I am the bread of life. Whoever comes to me will never go hungry, and whoever believes in me will never be thirsty.'" NIV

Philippians 4:11-13: "I am not saying this because I am in need, for I have learned to be content whatever the circumstances. I know what it is to be in need, and I know what it is to have plenty. I have learned the secret of being content in any and every situation, whether well-fed or hungry, whether living in plenty or in want. I can do all this through him who gives me strength." NIV

Grace of Heritage

Versailles, Indiana
1938

For from fullness, we have all received grace upon grace.
- John 1:16 ESV

Versailles Elementary stood tall and serene on the west side of our little town. Built of custom-glazed vanilla brick, its windows reminded me of a checkerboard. The building was constructed in 1938 by philanthropist James Tyson, who also created a matching library and church a few yards away. This triad made up a predominant geographical space of my childhood. These buildings, within five minutes' walking distance of one another, were the anchor for educational, social, and spiritual conventions. The trio created continuity in all areas of my life. School, Library, and Church were all built of the same vanilla-colored glazed terra cotta brick. Philanthropist James H. Tyson, the co-founder of Walgreens, left his mark on our community.

James H. Tyson (1856-1941) was born 106 years before I was in Versailles, Indiana. He was the son of William and Eliza. Tyson was one of seven children, not unusual for this era. As a young man, Tyson learned the printing trade at the local newspaper and bought a printing company in Chicago in 1890. Tyson lived in the same boarding house as the famous Charles Walgreen and became friends with him. Today, every city and town seems to have a corner dotted with a drug store with Charles' last name in red gleaming letters.

Charles Walgreen owned one drugstore and wanted to buy another one. James Tyson let him borrow $1500 to purchase the second store, and by 1927, the number had grown to 110 stores. At the time of writing this, there are over 9,000 Walgreens stores in existence. James Tyson remained a business partner with Charles and was given shares of the company as part of their business agreement. The town of Versailles became the benefactor of this boarding house friendship.

James Tyson's Temple is the physical place that began the faith journey for this not-quite-so-famous pharmacist to make an investment. Not in brick and mortar *or* mortar and pestle. But in kingdom work. The Tyson fund today still benefits the town each year and its proceeds are distributed by the Board of Trustees on Tyson's birthday, September 14th.

The church building, a two-story Art-Deco style building, was built in 1937 in white glazed brick and terra cotta. Not a single nail was used in its construction. Influenced by Tyson's travels to Europe and the Middle East, he eliminated wood in the church's construction, except for the furnishings. The building is called a temple because "hammers were not heard" in its construction, a reference to Israel's Holy Temple.

James Tyson had a vision to build a church for others to experience God. He dedicated it "to the Glory of God." What Tyson did has changed generations. Not everything that happens in our lives is just because of us; there are many influences that have shaped society. This is prevenient grace. My pathway is not shaped by myself alone. The steps I take, the things I encounter, and the people who come into my pathway are guided by a light from generations long ago. Tyson's grand gesture of generosity has drawn many people toward God, creating a quiet circle of wisdom within my reach. Mr. James Tyson bestowed much more than a physical building to my hometown. The generosity and humility of a long line of witnesses govern the trajectory of life in hidden ways.

Tyson Temple.
A grand name for a grand edifice.
It is a small building in scope of size.

It is fabulous in the scope of architecture.

The hidden graces that poured out across the generations are innumerable. I grew up in a small town far from the halls of academia, yet God taught me theological truths without a single commentary on the shelf and no Hebrew or Greek scholar within miles. In part, this was due to the generosity of a man who had lived many years before I was born.

The heart of a small-town printer significantly shapes lives, even 100 years later.
Grace and grace and more grace.
My God is the same as Mr. Tyson's God. As Moses' God.
For it is by grace you have been saved…so no one can boast," writes the apostle Paul. An eternal truth. I cannot boast. Mr. Tyson did not boast, Moses did not boast, I will not boast.

A good half-truth: "Faith is better caught, not taught" comes to mind. Yes, I was taught many things. However, many shared their ordinarily extraordinary lives, and I caught their faith.

Don't be afraid, for I am with you.
 Don't be discouraged, for I am your God. Isaiah 41:10

"But by the grace of God I am what I am…" - 1 Corinthians 15:10a

The Grace of God's House

1960s-1970s

*"I was **glad** when they said unto me, let us go into the house of the Lord." - Psalm 122:1*

The church building was where I first met Jesus.

No one who ever meets Jesus ever stays the same.

The building is often a visual for my God-moments.

I see the people, hear the music, and feel the warmth of fellowship when the swirl of His presence is upon me. God alone creates beauty, and every good and perfect gift comes from Him. A church, or even a building with architectural interests, brings me to a state of wonder.

I adore hymns permeating my pores. It is scientifically known that rhythmic sound synchronizes brain waves, and music affects serotonin and dopamine levels that influence mood. Once a song begins not only do I hear the notes, the words, and the chords, there is a visceral vibrancy that occurs from the audible. The call to worship, a rhythm of corporate prayer guiding, and a gospel lesson instructing are life-affirming. When I approach wearily from a week of the world's distractions, physical and mental, I am awakened and leave renewed. But it's not just the people that bless my heart; it's the building itself–it was built with love and to glorify God.

Tyson's Temple features a Corinthian-style front portico, a round-arched entry, and curved bays with ribbon windows. An open lattice spire of cast aluminum sits atop the building, and a cross adorns the tip-top. The building is a shelter: here, a preacher, a choir, and a people gather to worship the eternal God. Tangibles bow to the Intangible.

The church has a copper roof: lead covering copper covering concrete. At the time it was built in 1937, there was only one other roof like it in the United States. Its steps of pearl pink granite were a reflection of what Tyson saw as "mansions above."

Every Wednesday, I would walk from school to choir practice at Tyson Temple. The five-minute walk took me to the towering front bronze doors of the church; I would tug to open them up and run down the steps to the cool basement with Italian marble, where snacks, cookies, and other homemade snacks were served. Then we began singing, a church building providing elegant shelter for the equipping of another generation to advance the gospel.

A rounded seal above the church door states, "Glory to God." The filigreed cast iron steeple rises 100 feet above the ground of the Art Deco masterpiece. All this was extraordinarily ordinary to me. I walked in; I walked out. The beauty infused my daily life quite silently, seamlessly.

On Sunday, Mother would drive us into town, and we would all enter under the "Glory to God" inscription to gather for Sunday School. Then, we went up to the sanctuary for worship. I expected to be greeted each week by this most fabulous place on earth. After all, it was where I met the God of the universe.

James Tyson built my church in memory of his mother, Eliza. The ceiling is painted with the constellation of the night of his mother's death, with the North Star fashioned in gold leaf. The lovely artwork is illuminated with light from wall fixtures. It was intriguing to gaze at this as a youngster during worship services. I look upon this today and know this night of "death" was a night of life eternal for Eliza.

The building encompassed the One Who loved me first, and I grew to love Him there. I not only met God and worshiped him at my church but there was also a deep sense of belonging fulfilled in the physical building itself. The God I met was invisible, yet mysteriously there. Can God's presence be in a smell? There was a clean smell that radiated a power words cannot make known. I did not hear God. I did not see God.

There is a trend today where people seek to hear from the Lord directly so they can sound very authoritative, I believe. I may sound better if I were to write, "The Lord told me" or "I know God was present in this physical church because A and B and C." However, I cannot do this. The primary way God communicates with us today is through his Word. In this building, I heard his Word. As Jesus promised his disciples, "The Spirit of Truth…will guide you into all truth." John 16:13 There is a phrase used to energize discipleship: "God does not want you to *go* to church; he wants you to *be* the church."

In going to the church, I was learning how to *be* the church.

The Grace of Art

1960s

The Jesus picture.

Jesus was always there.

The large, framed man Jesus print hung above the Sunday School altar. The Jesus picture measured about four feet tall by two and a half feet wide. Every Sunday morning, I walked through the doors into the white-glazed brick church, descended the curved bay stairs, and was welcomed into cool surroundings and His presence. There was his picture on the wall.

As far as I was concerned, Jesus could see in and through all who entered that room. No act went unnoticed. Jesus Christ, the Savior of the universe, inhabited our church basement as much as I did.

He was with us every week as we gathered in the first row of tiny chairs for the Sunday School opening.

It was as if He, *Warner Sallman's Jesus,* was there in our Sunday School room. His eyes gently watched over my Sunday School scene. He witnessed all of it: scraping chairs on the floor, the "Deep and Wide" song with motions, dimes in our pockets for the offering, scuffed patent leather shoes, girls whispering in the back. It was as if Jesus himself were unrolling the scroll and teaching us the lesson through songs, Bible reading, and prayer. Jesus was the force behind all of us–in every chair. A child's mind thinking. Jesus the quarterback. Jesus is a point guard. He is in charge. I can count on him. He directs and knows the game plan because He does see me.

Grown up me knows The Force is bigger than Star Wars, the NFL, and the NBA combined.

He is the Good Shepherd- he saved the one lost sheep out of 100, he healed a man who had been blind from birth, and he enabled Peter to walk on water. Jesus is my Batman—knowing where I should go and when I need help, and I will be his Robin, exclaiming, "Holy gamole-y." You've got this, Lord!

This small-town church taught me the small things that provided large foundations in faith by inspiring active observation, encouraging communication with adults and peers, and relying on Biblical truths to generate these ideas.

The framed *Warner Sallman Head of Christ, Jesus (WSJ),* gazed upon me in the basement of Tyson United Methodist Church and became *my* own image of Grace, God, Jesus, Love, Power, Authority, and Who dwelled among us. It evoked an understanding of who Jesus was and provided sensory detail to God. Sallman's Jesus is a portrait headshot, much like Clark Gable would have done in 1940 when it was painted. Jesus is portrayed as masculine, yet warm with a not-quite-smile gaze, and has an ethereal space around him reminiscent of a photography studio setting. The use of light in this painting evokes power, faithfulness, love, and holiness. My love of words—Scripture—is enhanced with this visual. I saw a bearded, long-haired man with brown eyes looking peacefully, strongly into the distance. I guess in the original, the eyes are blue (maybe the church basement has dimmed our copy), and the skin on Jesus is more white than some people think it should be, but I didn't see color; I saw the radiance and his demeanor. Jesus was strong. Jesus was peaceful. Jesus was seeing.

 A single image can spark our curiosity or influence our consciousness and make a lasting impression. It can spur change and even shape history. By faith, we can sense God's presence 2000 years later in an artist's print hanging on a wall. Art can be the link between the resources of the unseen world and this temporary one.

Warner Sallman's Jesus (WSJ) is in a line of greats. Sallman painted for his audience—Swedish believers but has influenced many more, much like artists of old.

The Healing of the Paralytic is believed to be the oldest painting of Jesus in the world that still exists. It is a clear depiction of Christ, dating from around 200 A.D. It is in Syria in an ancient church. I think, "Where the heck is Syria located?" It's East of Jordan, west of Iraq, and south of Turkey. Damascus is the main city, and a small part borders the Mediterranean Sea. The leader is a hot mess, and there has been unrest there for years and years. BUT – this country, along with its bordering "friends," is the crucible of faith history. Imagine someone in Syria reading this and saying, "Where the heck is Versailles, Indiana?"

There are images of Jesus in the catacombs in Rome. I know where Rome is and have toured a few of the catacombs. For 2000 years, humanity has desired a two-dimensional depiction of Jesus to assist their faith journey. Even today, I have a crayon hand-colored Jesus keychain, which Allison made me, that reminds me of Who is with me...

Art may seem like an escape from reality, but it inevitably leads one into a face-to-face encounter with reality.

The Grace of Music

Versailles, Indiana
1960s

Every week during Sunday School opening, Mrs. Holman gathered the throng of Sunday Schoolers together in front of the Savior's likeness. She was one of Jesus' ambassadors to execute the Sunday duties. Her gray hair and navy blue dress were adorned with a necklace, and I thought it was a standard uniform for every Sunday school director. Mrs. Holman waited patiently for every child to come forward for the singing of "My Bible and I…" There was never impertinence.

We gathered in rows of folding chairs under the gentle gaze of Jesus to sing our opening songs. There were several songs to choose from, and we all knew them by heart. The assembled children would stand in front of the Jesus painting and chirp, sing, or mumble the Sunday selection.

We recited together:

"Lord of the sunlight
Lord of the starlight
Lord of the seasons
Teach me to know;
How best to love thee
How best to serve thee
Midsummer's flowers
Or winter's snow."
Amen

My friend Bonnie sang the songs at my side. Bonnie, a year older than me, was tall with brown curly hair. Like me, she had glasses (I got contacts in 8th grade). She was very smart, and I admired her demeanor: she was serious, attentive, kind and always ready to acknowledge the younger kids. Bonnie, her sister Connie, Natalie, my sister Amy, Donnie, Susan, Scott, Kevin, Linda, Alvin, Brian Todd, Eddie, Kendall, Eric, Lori, Kerri, Nicki, and I… we would all gather to sing the songs before dispersing to our classes. The songs were more than music—they brought levity to the morning and a sense of inward joy.

In those folding chairs, we worshiped God the Father, Jesus the Son, and the Holy Spirit. The songs taught us that the Lord is our strength, Jesus loves us, and he is all-powerful. We learned we were being made holy and that we had an assurance of eternal life. We were riding the *Happy Day Express*. We knew that EVERY single prayer was being heard because "God answers prayer in the morning… God answers prayer at noon…." I did not know these songs were theology lessons. We loved to sing *The B-I-B-L-E, Joy Joy Joy, Jesus Loves Me, The Happy Day Express, Keep Your Heart In Tune, This Little Light of Mine, Saved Every Day of the Week, Into My Heart, Zacchaeus, One Door, Welcome*

Song, Jesus Bids Us Shine, I'll Be a Sunbeam, Fishers of Men, Happy All the Time... The songs were putting language to my Jesus. My personal Jesus. He was with me. Each lyric was an apologetic.

Warner Sallman's Jesus knew me and eye-spied me in this building. He later called me to play piano. "Can you play for the opening of Sunday School? It is only a few songs, and the kids don't care if you make a mistake. You have to be here every Sunday or find a substitute if you are gone. Remember, I will be here if anything goes sideways," he said.

OK–Yes– there was an ambassador with skin that officially asked me, but it was definitely WSJ that was in charge of the prompting. Like Moses, I suggested someone with better skills. In God-like fashion, answering the King of the Universe's request (even when from an ambassador) is met with "I don't think so." The noodling didn't work.

I began to play the songs in the Sunday School opening. These songs helped me learn the traditions of the faith: The Apostle's Creed, baptism, Holy Communion, liturgical practices and forms. There was a historic deposit of the living Christian tradition poured over me.

From the beginning, the church tradition remained alive in my heart through common worship. All the actions of my life flowed from that worship. Lifestyles are formed, but not without the foundations of what I knew from worshiping Jesus. I cultivated the habit of thinking of Him often, but our minds are flighty, so I would sing this in my mind during the week:

"Glory be to the Father and to the Son and to the Holy Ghost

As it was in the beginning, is now and ever shall be

World without end, Amen, Amen."   (Gloria Patri, the Lesser Doxology 2nd Century)

It helped me focus. It enabled me to redirect to a larger view when challenged.

I had no idea it could begin on small wooden chairs in a basement in front of Jesus himself.

All the while, the Warner Sallman Jesus smiled upon us.

"But Jesus said, "Let the little children come to me. Don't stop them because the kingdom of heaven belongs to people who are like these children." - Matthew 19:14

The Grace of Liturgy

The bounty of growing up in the church and having a front-row seat for many years is that you are exposed to many sermons. Through all of them, at least a couple of sermon arrows hit me. Much of the benefit was simply being there. Being present. Being with The One. I had a deep sense of God being there. Why wouldn't He be? Omniscient, Omnipresent, and Omnipotent meant that God was in my time zone, attended my church, observed my religious traditions, and that His experience was my experience. I knew He loved me. He loved it when I loved it. When I disliked it, he was displeased.

As I sat in the far-right corner of Pew One at Tyson for easy access to the piano (which I played alongside the organist), I heard sermons, prayers, creeds, songs, and the sound of children prattling. The minister, the Lay Leader, the liturgists, the choir members, and the ushers fulfilled their duties with great care. Congregants worshiped God with reverence. Jesus Christ, Lord of all, was interceding for us–all of us–even the Baptist worshipers just a few blocks away.

Jesus was the central and defining figure in my spiritual life. He was God revealed. The Trinity was not equally represented in my realm. God was just too God. I assumed The Holy Spirit was there, but I could not put a perfect visual to this wispy form. Perhaps starry sprinkles around everyone and everything? Jesus brought into the open what I could not have figured out for myself. He was God among us–and He was God alongside me. Acting, listening, and seeing all that was going on in my world. A New Revised Standard Bible was gifted to every third grader at Tyson, and the Jesus I found within enabled me to take seriously who I was and where I was going. He had skin on him, at least for thirty years he did, and now he sits at the right hand of God with jaunts to help his people. Just me, ordinary me, would not play piano in front of a crowd. Jesus and Me: we did it together—there was no epiphany. He "dwelled among us" in ancient times, and He was with me without fanfare. He was with others as well.

Even though I could not give vision to the sparkly one, it was apparent the Spirit was alive and well in the sanctuary because this small church kept the flame burning. Amid small congregations and less-than-stellar mortal leadership, the people gathered to worship. I dearly wished at times the Spirit would move the dragging sermon along or help me through the song with three sharps that I was playing for the next hymn. These contemplations were silent prayers offered to the heavenlies. They were Sunday front-row meditations.

Sundays came, Sundays went:

Two Hymns,
The Doxology,
Gloria Patri,
Sermon and Prayer
Year A,
Year B,
Year C…

Those in the pew knew the routine.
It was beautiful; it was soothing. It was inspiring.
It comforted. It guided. It protected.

The doctrine was infused into my head by repetition. Did it penetrate into my being? Into the *whole of it?* It is one thing to have a doctrine embedded in the brain; it is another to have it be the controlling aspect of the *faith* by which you live. Far from loving God in return for His benefits, I needed to love Him even if there were no punishment to avoid or reward to gain. The purity of love expressed towards the Creator causes freedom and delight. I was not there—but almost. The pulsating of who Warner Sallman's Jesus was entered my blood… but it didn't enter my heart until later.

Oh, how I did love Jesus. Justification by faith was never questioned. It was a given. I had faith in God. He had sent his Son–I was all in.

But the *fullness* of His love, mercy and grace did not embrace me–yet.

The Grace of Rhythm

1978

"Walk with me and work with me—watch how I do it. Learn the unforced rhythms of grace." Matthew 11:29, The Message

We flutes were always in the front row.

I looked up, and Mr. Holdsworth quickly strode into the high school band room. As he passed his glass-wrapped office and walked towards the music stand, a room full of distracted students suddenly turned forward. I leaned over toward my fellow musician, and we wrapped up our conversation. Then, the squawking and rattling of teens blowing into woodwinds and brass instruments began. Percussionists tinkered on the top ring of the music room.

We tested the instructor at times, but he was all in from the first downbeat. I was center-right as the conductor looked upon us. I could view the clarinets, saxophones, and some trumpets. The trombones lined up behind my right ear. Mr. Holdsworth conducted our high school band and trained us to be versatile. We were a marching band for the summer months, a pep band for basketball season, and a concert band for the rest of the school year.

After the usual warm-up, he snapped his fingers and raised his arms to indicate, "Instruments up!" Mr. Holdsworth bellowed, "Saturday in the Park."

We instantly sank into the syncopated rhythm that innervates this song. The tune infused energy into the pace of the midday fourth period, right after lunch. We loved it.

Jamming to Chicago's pop hit in the 1970s was heaven on earth. The sound of Chicago's "Park" made everyone in the room loose. It was our jazzy, cool, morphing, blended-together being. We were the generation that wore bright colors and Chic jeans by H.I.S. with contrast stitching. The band room was full of bell-bottom jeans, peasant blouses, striped shirts, and Farrah Fawcett hair. "I think it was the fourth of July," ribboned through my head as I played my Gemeinhardt.

On Wednesday evenings, Mr. Holdsworth directed the church choir with the same downstroke that he used on weekdays at school. Mrs. Holdsworth played the piano alongside him. Mrs. Price was at the organ, and Mrs. Westmeyer sang harmony. The tempo of my life was given character and shape by these masters of grace. I learned about long marriages, words of faith, old friendships, and opportunities to remember. The poet Czeslaw Milosz, who won the Nobel Prize in Literature in 1980, wrote that our planet was characterized by a bewildering "refusal to remember." "Remember these things, O Jacob and Israeli, for you are my servant; I formed you." Isaiah 44:21 The rhythm of my life is bound by particulars: particular people, stories, and places.

Saturday in the Park was in the same motion as Amazing Grace. Mr. H encompassed his God-gig with energy and ease. Again, snapping his fingers together, he would look over our group, give the nod and the downbeat, and start our church choir warbling.

Grace poured over me through small, ordinary moments. If God revealed all of his glory and absolute power in one instant, we would be shattered. We could not tolerate God's presence directly. So God reveals himself to us through ordinary circumstances and fleeting glimpses of his power and beauty.

The vessels God used to spread unmerited favor were disguised: they were sitting next to me in the band, teaching me in the choir, working as Sunday school teachers and unrecognized as family members. In church speak, "disciples" of Jesus swirled unceremoniously around me, delivering the unexpected and underserved divine favor. Mysteriously, Saturday in the Park and Amazing Grace had the same rhythm and unity in my life. There was no division. One in a tiered high school band room and another in a historic golden-enameled choir loft.

Life under the sun and life under heaven came a little closer together on Sunday morning. A small-town Midwest school band rocked the music room while the church choir sang a song on Sunday that lifted the congregation. The heavenlies heard both of these with joy.

The Grace of Legacy

1891

James Tyson, the benefactor of our town, had an aunt named Nancy (his mother's sister) who died in April of 1891. Her obituary was placed in the local newspaper (which I still subscribe to). I compared the words of her obituary to the current-day obituaries in the paper today and found a sharp contrast. Today, even people of faith rarely state their love of family or God with this much flourish.

In Memoriam

2 April 1891
Versailles Republican

"In fond remembrance of our dear mother, Nancy Smock, who died at her home near Cross Plains on Sunday, 8 March 1891, aged 70 years & 3 months. She became a member of M.E. Church when but 11 years old & has lived a faithful member till the last, and also a faithful mother. She leaves 3 sons & 2 daughters, 4 sisters & a host of other relatives & friends to mourn their loss. She was perfectly conscious & realized that her summons had come. She was fully prepared & ready to go without a shadow of a doubt for the future. The pearly gates of her heavenly home were open to her vision & while she said her last fond words of love & counsel to her loved ones here & heard their sobs of grief, her ear caught the voice of her loved ones just across the river, welcoming her home. Her remains were laid tenderly to rest in the cemetery at Cross Plains on 10 March 1891 in the presence of a large concourse of friends & neighbors. We have laid thy form in the grave to rest, Thy purse white soul is now among the blessed, the place now is vacant around the hearthstone, and our hearts are so sad since our Mother has gone. Oh, the pain that we felt as we watched day by day, The dear lovier Mother fast fading away. Yet, we hoped against hope, praying to God to restore Our mother to health once more. But He, for some purpose, saw fit to remove. Our loved one from earth to mansions above. Now she is wearing a bright starring crown, Prepared by the Savior for his loyal & His own. Some day we shall meet them if found worthy, a crown fitted with gem & jewels rare."

This is the culture of daily life that influenced James Tyson. In those days, it was an honor to grieve the loss of a loved one and articulate it through words. What a legacy this man left behind. His entire family was deeply devoted to God. These treasures have been passed down over the years.

Tyson loved God, and he also loved Indiana. His legacy is remembered. In the words of Tyson's contemporary:

Ain't God good to Indiana
Folks, a feller never knows
Just how close he is to Eden
Till, sometimes, he ups and goes
Seekin' fairer, greener pastures
Than he has right here at home
Where there's sunshine in th' clover,
An' there's honey in th' comb;
Where th' ripples on th' river
Kind o' chuckle as they flow--
Ain't God good to Indiana?
Ain't he fellers? Ain't he though?

Ain't God good to Indiana?
Seems to me He has a way
Gettin' me all out o' humor
Just to see how long I'll stay

When I git th' gypsy feelin'
That I'd like to find a spot
Where th' clouds ain't quite so restless
Or th' sun don't shine so hot
But, I don't git far, I'll tell you,
Till I'm whisp'rin soft and low:
Ain't God good to Indiana?
Ain't he fellars? Ain't he though?

Ain't God good to Indiana?
Other spots might look as fair.
But they lack the soothin' somethin'
In th' Hoosier sky an' air.
They don't have that snug up feelin'
Like a mother gives a child;
They don't soothe you, soul an' body
With their breezes soft an' mild,
They don't know th' joys of heaven
Have their birthplace here below;
Ain't God good to Indiana?
Ain't He fellars? Ain't He though?

-William Hershell, (1873-1839) Indiana Journalist

The Grace of Lifelong Friendship

Holton, Indiana
1874

Friendships can last a lifetime and are God's gift to us. The bonds of generations past reveal God's grace going before us. God does not drop a new Bible from heaven on every generation. He intends one generation to teach the next generation to draw near to God. God personally seeks everyone through Scripture and the preceding generation: grace imparted horizontally and vertically.
"One generation shall praise Your works to another, and shall declare your mighty acts." - Psalm 145:4

The small autograph book is bound in a navy, light blue, and charcoal filigree cover. It has a small, worn picture of a celestial city engraved at the top. I can make out two castles, a bridge, and a tree. Anna signed her name on the inside cover in a beautiful script: Ann M. Flick, Holton, Ind. Embellished with a curly image.

This family heirloom autograph book belonged to my father's great-aunt, Anna Flick (1874-1957), from Holton, Indiana. In the autograph book, across the generations, come the reminders of the friendships she built many years ago.

Every autograph is in cursive. They are not in chronological order. Here are some excerpts of the entries:

Friend Anna,
Remember me in friendship
Remember me in love
Remember me forever
Till we meet in heaven above
Your friend A.B.
New Marion, February 27, 1889

Dear Anna:
I write these simple lines for thee,
Whence you see them, think of me.
Your friend,

Maggie Denny, Jan 31-18

Friend Anna,
When you get old and ugly,
As most of people do,
Remember that your old friend
Is getting ugly too.
Your Friend, Lula Rofs
New Marion Ind.

Dear Anna,
In the struggle of life, meet its difficulties bravely, solve its problems carefully;
Improve its opportunities diligently. Then, at last, thou wilt approach thy grave
serenely, and in the resurrection morn thou wilt rise triumphantly. Your Friend
Anna B. Naylor
Winter of '89 & '99
New Marion, Ind.

Dear Anna,
I wish you health
I wish you wealth
I wish you joy below.
I wish you heaven after death
What could I wish you more.
M.N.
New Marion Jan. 1889

Dear Anna
Go thou in life's fair morning,
Go in the bloom of youth
And buy for thine adorning
The precious pearl of truth
Your friend Lena Gabel
New Marion, Ind 1893

Dear Anna
May the morn of your life be bright and joyous
The noontide peasfull(sic) happy
The sunset gloriously hopeful
Is the wish of your Sister
Louisa
Holton, Ind Dec 24, 1888

Friend Anna,
Remember me when
Far, far of.
Where the Wood chucks
Die with the hooping
Cough.
Flora Fox
Holton, Ind.

Cousin Anna:
May you ever be happy
Harry P. Custer
Nebraska, Ind 6.2.1893

After I discovered these treasures in the autograph book, I also found a sweet, handwritten note written by my daughter, Allison, when she was little. One hundred years, five generations, separate Anna and Allison. Two authors who reflected on the heartbeat of friendship and companionship. And I was touched to realize that my daughter chose me, her mother, to be the friend and companion she honored in her note.

Allison's journal
age 7
Written in cursive
Circa 2000

Dear Mom,
I love you, and I hope you feel the same for me too.

The way you walk, the way you talk, it is so unique (sic) and good,
If I could, I would spend all day with you because of your great person.
I love you a ton,
I do not want you to ever go out of my site
your soul is silky white.
I love you so much.

My heart smiled when I read this. Allison fills my life with special things that bring radiance. Her laughter penetrates a room with her vibrancy. Her words reveal her sweet soul. My prayers and words will always swirl around my lovely daughter.

"Friendship is unnecessary, like philosophy, like art... it has no survival value. Rather, it is one of those things that give value to survival." – C.S. Lewis

Grace of Motherhood

The days they were born

September 21, 1989

Snippets of color remain embedded in my memory. The maternity jumpsuit I wore that my mother made for me, white shorts with green stripes on top. David loaded the dishwasher before we went to the hospital that morning. I was induced for our firstborn. The kitchen linoleum brown and crème, countertops laminate white. Our last moments of "two."

The white and yellow tiny room in the hospital. Yes, I know it was yellow. As soon as the contractions started – just white, that is the color of total focus for me. Beforehand–we had our personal moments that I recall as–humorous or at least not like you would see in a television movie.

"David, do you remember?" I asked. His recollection was not quite the same, but he did comment that mine was valid, but maybe the pain had skewed my sentiments. The doctor induced me and said it might take a while. You left and went to work and brought a sandwich and a friend back, and by that time, I was in labor. I didn't know whether to laugh or cry. It was happening so fast… We attended the hospital's labor/delivery classes, where we were told, "Breathing and counting will alleviate pain."

I was young and I believed the nurse. In the short labor I had, I seriously thought I should be the guest speaker next session at these birth classes and tell them the truth: "You will think you are dying because there is so much pain, but you are not dying. Be ready for the experience because it is worth it, BUT know there will be black-out pain. Forget breathing; guttural screams may overtake your body."

After a swirling labor, I held my infant son. You cannot go back once you have this experience. The bond of love is unbroken for eternity. Life to life. Forever.

There was no regular sleep for a long while with Austin. At one-year-old, he knew thirteen words. He loved walking and talking, running and being with family. Just not sleeping.

Before I had Austin, I was driving, and there was a full moon glowing in the sky. I came around the corner, almost home, and I was breathless by the magnificence of this moon. It was not audible, but I clearly heard a word: Special. It was breathed through the celestial brightness of the moon, voiceless yet distinct and clear to my understanding. My children would be special. I had a very calm and peaceful sense come over me. I knew it was a sign to me personally. Not for grandeur or significance in the world but for God's use. "Special." That is it. No specifics. I have trusted this sign, although I questioned it, too. Do I need to do something to assist this, Lord? Amusing question. God needs help? If he does, he knows how to get ahold of me. A big bright moon.

November 18, 1993

I was tired all day. David arrived home from work, and I sat on the sofa while he made supper for Austin. The warm glow of light in our home penetrated the early evening darkness. The wooden walls of our log home were honey-colored, and the towering center-room rock fireplace was blazing. I watched the flames lick the logs which eased my dull backache, being warm and comfortable while David and Austin were doing their nightly routine. Our last night of "three." Around midnight, we left for the hospital. Another "funny" thing occurred with Allison's birth. We dropped off Austin at Uncle Jeff and Aunt Amy's, and David sped to the hospital a couple of miles away. Being thoughtful, he dropped me off at the front door. I am in full-blown labor by this time. The front doors are locked with a sign: "After midnight, please use Emergency Room Entrance Only." I turned around and found myself standing there alone because David had left in such a hurry to park the car. There was a long walk to the ER doors. I knew it would be a bit before he was back from the parking lot behind the hospital, so I started the trek around the building. Nothing like a little hike before you give birth! The emergency room staff quickly had a wheelchair for me as David ran into the building. Up we go to Labor and Delivery.

The humor does not end there. I can use the word 'humor' after thirty years. The hospital staff is polite and quickly gets me settled in a room. Since I had a natural childbirth with Austin, I wanted to give an epidural a try this time. In fact, I was uncompromising on this. The doctor and nurse checked me, and they indicated the anesthesiologist would be in for the epidural.

Dr. So and So, the anesthesiologist, arrives in minutes. He takes a look at my spine and says, "No problem." Then Dr. So and So and David start chatting. I mean chatting. Sports, weather…whatever. A few minutes pass. A few more. I look at them in their casual, relaxed form, chuckle, and say, "Hello…how about the epidural?" A long walk to the ER door, and now I am waiting for a social hour to be over for pain relief! David says he was establishing a good vibe with him—after all, he was going to stick a large needle in my spine. And a little after 4 am our daughter was born.

We were now four. I could not believe how beautiful she was. It took a few hours to know what to name her…this perfect little girl.

I was wrong about both children in predicting the sex. We did not find out ahead of time. It was very exciting not knowing. There is beauty in mystery and anticipation. The anticipation that mere mortals cannot control.

Allison slept. At age one she liked board books in her bed. She still likes books in her bed—ask her husband, Brandon!

The gifts my children have were evident at once.

A reader and an eloquent speaker. Allison works well with written words, and Austin speaks powerfully and persuasively.

Guiding Grace

1979

"Not often, but every once in a while, God brings us to a major turning point –a great crossroads in

our life…" –Oswald Chambers

Where am I going? What to do? Mom and Dad were asking what college I was going to attend. Friends were starting to select their destinations after high school.

These questions resonated deeply with me as a seventeen-year-old.

College? For me, the answer was, "Of course." Even though neither of my parents graduated from college, I was determined to be university-bound and not stay in Versailles.

I was on my own to figure out what major I should pursue. I knew my parents were not paying for "finding myself" and experimenting with different majors in college. Gap years had not come into vogue, so I had to decide immediately and not change my mind. This was not going to be a target practice college experience. I had one shot at college and had to do it in the allotted four years.

There were no guidance counselors at my high school to lead me in one direction or another. I take that back: There was a guidance counselor. Her guidance: she told me to take a #2 pencil to the SAT exam.

As I prepared to take the SAT, I was nervous. The only aptitude testing in high school I recall was the one Armed Forces test you had to take, and that test did not go well. There was a section with boxes drawn visually unfolded, and you had to tell them what it looked like when folded up. "Ridiculous," I thought.

I asked Ricky Estelle about that section afterward.

He said, "The easiest part of the test. I had those done in less than thirty seconds."

I thought I was doomed. Neither of my parents graduated from college. How was I going to do it?

All my friends went to a different SAT testing site. There was only one other student from my school at my location. Jim and I nodded at one another. There were no distractions. Maybe it was a good thing. I did pretty well.

The various jobs I had held through high school did not lead to an epiphany about a future career. The usual teacher/nurse agenda was not hitting any buttons. I sent a note to NASA in 6th grade, and they responded with an official letter explaining what would happen to a glass of water when spilled in space, so I thought science was intriguing.

I had liked the sciences since freshman biology. Miss Engel, a new teacher, refined my interest in science, and I leaned into exploring this area more and more. Her enthusiasm and great organizational skills made me focus in a new way. The white folder filled with notes and drawings of cells is still vivid in my mind. It may even be in my box of "need to get rid of." An interest in pharmacy kept nagging me, but I hadn't decided where to attend school. Pharmacy would employ biology and chemistry, and the profession seemed to have a good mix of intellectual activity with the ability to have patient contact that mattered.

One day, when I went on a bike ride into town, entering the drug store, I walked along a magazine rack that flanked the right entry aisle as I headed back to pick up a prescription from Alan Smith, "Smitty," the owner and pharmacist.

Smitty had been there since the beginning of time. He handed out pills and dispensed daily doses of sports news, too. He was beloved by the townspeople. The physical building itself was small, but it never felt too cramped. The store met the needs of the community.

During my childhood summers, I would put water in a thermos, drop it in my basket attached to the front of my handlebars, and pedal my bicycle to town. Stopping in the drug store to get a candy bar, read comic books, and maybe visiting a friend or two in town would fill my day. Smitty had an impressive display of arrowheads at the pharmacy. The small-town space captivated me. Even if I had to wait my turn, I could look at the artifacts or listen to sports talk.

As I waited on the prescription, I knew being a pharmacist was the right choice. **Yes. That's it. I will become a pharmacist. It blended what intrigued me and what could make a difference in people's lives.**

"I will be applying this fall at Butler for their pharmacy program," I said to Smitty as I waited for the medicine. In between sports bites, he said, "That's great! I am sure you will love it." He was busy, but he took time to encourage me and acknowledge my direction in life. His response was non-committal in a way, yet it was still affirming.

I took the prescription and walked to the checkout. Smitty's wife was working the register.

"How are you doing?" she asked me while she made a change at the checkout.

I told her, "Fine. I am applying to Butler in the fall."

A look of disbelief came over her face. She wrinkled her face and exclaimed, "Pharmacy is very difficult. Do you mean you want to be a pharmacy tech, honey?"

There was a judgment in her tone and in the few words she spoke. I knew she had taken all the information she knew about me, my family, and her social position to make a remark that was inconsequential to her. Her remark had been condescending, and I felt its sting. She evaluated me as "not quite smart enough" for the rigors of becoming a pharmacist. In the half-second I had to respond, I felt a strength of conviction not of my own:

"No, Mrs. Smith, not a pharmacy tech, a pharmacist."

From that moment on, I never looked back. It wasn't to prove to her or anybody else, but I used this comment as a help and not to hinder. I needed to believe in myself and make a decision for myself. No one was going to make it for me.

I knew I was going to be a pharmacist. There are moments in life where God guides us in uncomplicated ways, but other moments are decisive and require action. I had plowed through several crossroads in life, without giving it much thought, which I think Mrs. Smith had taken into account—there are some family characteristics and attributes that every small town knows. I suppose she believed in generational sin, but I digress. There are things that remain unspoken when the last generation's sin has been rebuked and repented of. When I approached the turning point, there must have been an angel guarding me, making sure I made the right turn.

Warner Sallman's Jesus was hanging on the wall just one block over from the pharmacy. He was always with me, always guiding me. God recognized my limitations long before I was aware of them. He carefully led me along a gentle path through experiences that gradually prepared me for the next step. Whether at the pharmacy on a Friday or at church on Sunday morning, Jesus was there. The icon, as well as the Messiah. I depended on that presence even though I did not fully know who that guiding companion was.

The Grace of Lovely Words

"The mind of the wise makes their speech judicious…" - Proverbs 16:23a

Words have woven long ribbons through my life, constructing continuity. Reading Words, Admiring Words, Wincing at Words: some words go with you no matter where you are geographically, and some words stay behind. The exclamation "Good Gravy" does not resonate in Chicago but is solid in southern Indiana. I'll drink a "Coke" —meaning any carbonated soft drink. In high school, on a trip to Michigan, Jerilyn and I learned their Coke was "pop." Strange, we thought, to call your drink after a sound.

Sometimes, I dream about printed words tumbling out of the sky. The soft motion of the drifting text is pleasing yet frustrating. I struggle to read and reach them as they pass by endlessly in a swirling motion. Yet, I love the words. I don't want them to stop. Desiring to express gratitude for each word's power, I write and read, discuss and fuss. Words have energy with the ability to help and heal or hinder, harm, or humble. Consider the power we wield and impart with the endlessly swirling motion of words.

Words form the "soundtrack" that you play in your mind, as author Jon Acuff has efficiently phrased. The words you think of often will silently shape your habits and character. Acuf urges changing negative soundtracks into positive ones.

I like it when a *lovely* word is used, bringing a delightful fragrance to a conversation. I judge what is lovely, the recording in my mind goes off, and a beautiful fragrance filters through what is said. Each of us has our own set of lovely words that are personally precious to us.

Here are a few of my golden words:
Dandy: A word my grandpa and dad used; they were usually happy when saying it.

Bogie!: No one says this word like my daughter Allison after this score on the golf course.
Puzzling: David and I always cherished when Pastor Dripps used this word. We would look at one another and smile, pushing us to think deeper. Pastor Dripps would tilt his head and often put his forefinger to his lips as he would say this word.

Sacristy: Pronouncing it calms my mind and brings me to a higher place. And I like how it *feels* to pronounce it: Part of the word is "sacred," and part of the word is "Christ. There is a soft feel with great power in this word.

Words create scenes in my mind. The word "sacristy" makes my mind's movie start playing. I *see* focused clergy and committed lay people readying themselves for worship. I *hear* the clanging of the acolyte's candle lighter being retrieved from storage, along with the organist's prelude. I *smell* the wooden cabinets holding the choir director's music and the altar's candles, the communion cups and the altar adornments. I can *feel* the vestments – beautiful linen and fine embroidery, a stole woven of silk and an alb of wool. There is peace before exiting the sacristy into the sanctuary. Peace and Power.

"Words create worlds."- Rabbi Abraham Joshua Heschel

"In the beginning was the Word, and the Word was with God, and the Word was God..."
John 1:1

Proverbs 25:11: "A word softly spoken is like apples of gold in a setting of silver." ESV

The Grace of Wise Authors

✝

C.S. Lewis.
I read his books, and I consider our similarities.

Dear reader, don't turn from the page with laughter, thinking this comparison is preposterous! Don't we all align with the protagonist in our favorite book? We become participants with no barriers, like a secret shadow. I liked becoming Nancy Drew's friend as she solved mysteries, and I was telling Meg Murray to be careful in her adventure to find her father in *A Wrinkle in Time*. The fertility of imagination is unbridled. Freedom reigns, and my creative nature dictates the day. Let me explain some similarities between my humble life and Lewis's.

Lewis grew up in a rural setting. As for me, the small town where I grew up had one stoplight and two postal routes.

Jack had one brother; I have one sibling, a sister.

Jacksie, as Lewis called himself, constructed Animal Land (Boxen). In the same way, I created an imaginary place and imaginary friends who are still visible in my mind: Mr. Pendle and Margaret. Margaret's auburn hair is well-coiffed, and the emerald-green dress is classic. Mr. Pendle's suit is the finest charcoal-colored wool–could it have been a Brooks Brothers?

Lewis had a free-range life in his early years. I played with Little Kiddle dolls, jacks, and pick-up sticks. I rode my bike for miles and miles. We were both country fledglings nurtured in a safe nest.

Lewis's brother, Warren, was his "dearest and closest friend," and he also had many lifelong friends. Lewis and J.R.R. Tolkien belonged to "Inklings," an informal literary discussion group. This group would meet on Thursday evenings in Lewis' room or at a local pub, the Eagle and Child.

I formed lasting friendships on long bike rides and alongside my friends in school over the years. Like Lewis, I have gathered fellowship groups in my home to discuss theology and life. We founded one group, Friday Friends, based on the day we met. Like the Inklings, our group had no rules, officers, or formal agendas. And our group was all female–which mirrored the Inklings' all-male code.

Our meetings were not all serious either, just like Lewis's. It was said that Inklings would have competitions to see who could read aloud notoriously bad prose for the longest without laughing. In the same way, we Friday Friends laughed and cried together.

Maggie was our southern lady with deep prayer roots. Jeaninne would tell stories of her travels, and Meridee questioned perfectly and made me smile with her openness. We told life stories, we reasoned, and we compared and contrasted. We persuaded, told jokes, examined Scripture, debated political topics, and shared recipes.

I love the thought of mirroring a great scholar. Imagination and reality intersecting. I could make people come alive with my words! Maybe I could write like Mr. Lewis and experience things as deeply as he did. Mrs. Dent, my high school English teacher, would look upon this fantasy with a Cheshire cat smile and bring me back to reality: "Paula, how can you compare yourself to Clive Staples Lewis? He wrote forty books–many on apologetics–some of which are your favorites. He was a prodigy, a war hero, a theologian, and walked in the most prestigious circles…"

I may plead with her, though. "Mrs. Dent–it is my fantasy. May I compare our youths? May I indulge in a few moments of delight to say we are kindred spirits? Even if my group of friends is not the Inklings, it is still notable–after all, each relationship is valuable. And that is why I speak with you, my great teacher–in my mind after you have departed. I may not stand with Lewis in the confines of greatness, but I walk alongside him, drawing glimpses of light between the pages."

Mrs. Dent, I believe, would relent: "Very well. Walk with Mr. Lewis. But remember, do not tarry too long."

The Grace of Storge

✝

In his book, The Four Loves, C. S. Lewis describes "Love" in four different ways, based on the four words used in the Greek language for "love." The beautiful four words are: storge (empathy bond), philia (friendship bond), eros (romantic love), and agape (God's love).

Lewis describes Storge as the humblest and most widely diffused of the loves. It is modest and has a diffuse beginning. It unites people who happen to be dropped together by geography or household. It bonds child and parent and creates an affinity between people who are familiar with one another. In a word, it is brotherly love.

Growing up, we had a neighbor, Stanley "Butch" Evans. He worked for my dad occasionally, doing all types of things around the farm. He would work in the barn lot, always fixing something. Fixing everything.

He would drive by the house and wave.
And I rode the bus with his son, Wayne.
Butch was always "around." Wayne was always on the bus." There. Dependable. Present.

One horrible day, my sister's English sheepdog, Mopsy, was run over. As Mopsy lay in the road and we were weeping, Mom called down to see if Butch was home. He was and came to pick up Mopsy and took her to the vet, where she died. That day, we experienced the blessing of a merciful neighbor and friend during a most horrific event.

Over forty years passed. A wilderness traversed. I stood greeting friends and family at my father's memorial service. Suddenly, my legs buckled. Butch and Wayne were next in line. Time no longer had its reign. One glance at my friends and affection welled in my soul. They appeared as if they had walked up the sidewalk from the barn lot. I reached for Butch's hand and hugged him.

I said, "Wayne, it's so nice to see you."
"You remembered me," Wayne said quietly.

Storge.

Affection "is patient and kind. Love is not envious or boastful.

Love is "not puffed up." - 1 Corinthians 13:4, Darby Translation

Weathered brown skin, calm smile, creased eyes knowing the all-ness of my family: Dying dog, dusty barn lot, infidelities, sisters playing in the yard, sisters mourning dad. A neighbor and friend, a Light that glows without regard to time or distance, without regard to circumstance.

Butch and Wayne move through the line.
We traversed a wilderness that day and made it through.
"Faith dare the soul to go further than it can see." - William Clark, explorer.

Goodness and Mercy will follow me all the days of my life…

The Grace of Serendipity

✝

"…I have won and lost a dozen fortunes, killed many men, and loved only one woman…."
- a line from Robert Duvall's character, Hub, in Second Hand Lions

1984

In addition to Storge love, C.S. Lewis described Eros (Romantic), Phileo (Friendship) love, and Agape (Unconditional) love. In my life, these three types of love intertwined life. It was almost as if Lewis knew what was going to happen to me.

"Agape is not unconditional love. It is a love of the will rather than emotion." Lewis points out that God is love, but love is not God. God loves the sinner, but there is a special love for His redeemed people. He has an Eros-type desire and is filled with Agape love for them." These are notes from my journal recording C.S. Lewis' followers. I did not record this author's name.

Was it by chance that I asked for a ride home from the college campus that evening when I was a freshman? I made a seemingly odd after-dinner request to a senior boy who did not know me. Was it by chance that a handsome senior named David was in his dorm room that evening watching Monday night football with his friends when I had the courage to approach him?
 My odd request that evening elicited many gifts that none of us were looking for.
Some call it serendipity that I chanced to meet my future groom. I call it agape: a demonstration of the Divine Love that is ever with me. I am thankful for His ever-guiding hand and the blessing of serendipity, which I have known as Agape.

And our serendipity extended to others. My cousin Cathy and David's college roommate, Duke Hamm, met at our wedding. My sister, Amy, fell for David's friend, Jeff Liter, and another love turned into marriage.

Three weddings. Three loves. Three Devotions.

Love, three times over.
Phileo
Eros
Agape
Love poured over.

The One allowed three young women to be in the right place at the right time.
The One fought the battles and provided great riches for my daily needs.

"…apart from me, you can do nothing…" John 15

The Grace of Hospitality
✝

Come, you that are blessed by my Father, inherit the kingdom prepared for you…; for I was hungry and you gave me food, I was thirsty and you gave me something to drink, I was a stranger and you welcome me. – Matthew 25:34-35

Hospitality is an expression of love. People do not enter our lives to be manipulated but to enrich us by their differences and to be graciously received in the name of Christ.

My mother welcomed guests into our home. It was an open table concept: It might be set with silver and a punch bowl with cloth napkins and cake for birthday celebrations, anniversaries and graduations, hosting the local ladies' Home-Ec club, or a friend would stop by, and they would paint their nails at the kitchen table discussing daily life: kids, the lawn, the town, Tri-Kappa, and what's for dinner.

Why does this matter in my memory bank?

Early everything matters. Ask Chaim Potok, Frank McCourt, or Philip Yancy.

Mom was influenced by her Aunt Dot, who loved silver chafing dishes, although she didn't like cooking that much. Throw hot dogs and baked beans in silver, and it becomes gourmet. Mom, at over 80 years old, still has around thirty sets of cloth napkins to go with the twelve sets of china she has collected. Her home is decorated to convey taste, nostalgia, and comfort, welcoming the next guest.

51

The napkin does not fall too far from the table. Dishes, napkins, silver, tea sets, candle holders, crystal, table linens and serving trays are part of the Martha syndrome passed to me through the generations.

It is easy to be received by sincere hospitality. The work it takes to make a meal expresses God and makes Him real: Your guest is brought by an invitation, walking through a door to be warmly welcomed by the beauty of preparation, falling into conversation, and being fed food that satisfies demonstrates accommodation and reception with no barriers. Family dinners for thousands of years have had layers and layers of underlying dynamics radiating from each person, yet we break bread together, and it will go on until Christ returns. There have been times I have been the hostess, and there have been times I have been the recipient of gracious hospitality.

In St. Charles, there was often a gathering scheduled at our home. If it wasn't on the calendar, we often called the neighbors or friends for impromptu cookouts, and everyone would pitch in. Birthdays, graduations, and school team end-of-year parties were celebrated on the patio. If our fire pit could talk (or write), it could share interesting accounts of people's deepest thoughts. After a meal with friends on dark, cool nights, with the fire flickering skyward, words flow to the stars easily. Maybe it was the wine that we had…

On one of the last nights I lived in St Charles, Carol came over. David was gone–perhaps already in Arizona already--or traveling with work, and we sat on the patio glancing westward, enjoying the sunset. The sunset view is quite remarkable most evenings and didn't disappoint that night. We had a few tears, lamenting the distance that would be separating us before my move was permanent to Arizona, as it grew dark. Laughter crept in when tales of family fun times and our church endeavors. It was July, warm, without bugs biting. We talked about the dinners, lunches, and toasts we had experienced over the years. All the water under the bridge, some of the dry times and when the waters ran high.

Odd–how we ended up at the same place, same time…or is it? We met at church. We moved to St. Charles at the same time and joined Baker UMC with the same group, and our families were much alike. Each of us had an oldest son, and our daughters were the same age and had a lot of the same endearing personality characteristics. It was a bonus that our husbands were friends, too. Our relationship grew deeper over the years.

Suddenly, almost in our backyard, fireworks began to shower over us in a giant display of explosive colors. The striking loud noise blasted and rainbows would whirl, zoom, dart, dazzling our surroundings. The golf course our home bordered had an outing that day, and the grand finale was a spectacular fireworks display that lasted over twenty minutes.

We were breathless. This was hospitality on a new level. From above, not planned by the hostess but Heavenly. A grand farewell. Blessedness glowing: as we savored the moments together, the explosion of the fireworks triggered joy. The sizzling sounds and bright colors celebrated nostalgia. Laughter and "Ohhhhh"

Parting is such sweet sorrow.

"There is a time for everything,

and a season for every activity under the heaven

a time to plant and a time to uproot."- Ecclesiates 3:1,2b

There is no party like a God party.
That summer, after 27 years in St Charles, Illinois, we sold the house and moved to Arizona. When I fly back to Chicago, I will text Carol, "My flight arrives at noon tomorrow. Late lunch at Cooper's Hawk?" She will text back, "I'll have our regular booth ready. Maybe the guys will join us."
Our lunch will last until dinner.
Hospitality of the heart is about giving, not entertaining. Walking by faith and not by sight. Contributing to the needs of the saints, the weary, and your friend who longs for your smile.

The Grace of Family Tradition

1980s

"True love never dies. Doesn't matter if it's true or not. A man should believe in those things, because those are the things worth believing in."
-- Hub in the movie Secondhand Lions

Robert Duvall's Hub and I are different—I have not killed anyone. I have not won and lost any fortunes. But we are similar in one way: I have loved only one man. "Singular devotion" are the words that describe my relationship with my beloved husband.

In 1984, I married the love of my life, David Hall.

Shortly after we were married, I attended my first Hall family reunion in Cleveland. The Charles Hall family always gathered on Labor Day. It was a tradition that solidified their family relationships.

When I heard about the large-scale reunion, I was startled. My family is a small crew. My mother had one sister who died in 1991. My father had only one brother. For my side of the family, a family get-together is twelve people max.

David's family on his father's side had ten siblings who lived to adulthood. His mother had the same. The Halls didn't simply put one extra leaf on the table; they rented a state park venue or a residence that could host an open house outside with over one hundred people.

Traditions are an avenue to connect us to our past, create lasting memories, contribute to our identities, help us cope with loss, and provide an opportunity to communicate. This can be a street that is full of potholes or smoothly paved.

That first family reunion that we attended after we had kids was at a cousin's home with a fantastic large country yard in the suburbs of Cleveland. Granny Hall, David's grandmother and guest of honor, was still alive, and she was the center of everyone's attention.

As we drove up to the gathering, in this not-quite-rural nor a suburb home, there was a person in every nook and cranny and children running around. An RV was parked in the yard. Coolers were placed in various places with cans of soda and water. There were people sitting in lawn chairs. Some were in the kitchen, where food was being prepped. Some were in the house, and a few were in the driveway.

My first thought was, "Oh my Lord, I can't even begin to know who everyone is, but I will dive in and talk to Aunt Avanelle or cousin Jennifer, who are always friendly faces."

No one approached to welcome us. The Hall's clannish behavior was in full view. Teepees scattered with smoke rising from within would have been fitting for this gathering. There were family tribes huddled together with little room to encroach.

It was awkward for me but not so much for David. He was the prince of peace in the family. It was easy for him to interpose himself into one of the tribal huddles. He was one of the older cousins, beloved for his humility, resilience, confidence, responsibility, and athletic ability. Athletic ability was the most revered trait in the Hall family. He was a warrior in the tribe. A high school All-American—academics and baseball—and he had the backup of being a successful business executive as well.

David got busy with the men's Warrior crowd, and I filtered off to the women's groups. I was more of an onlooker than a family member. But it was a lovely end-of-summer day, and I enjoyed watching all the family units try to figure out who was who.

Then I saw the cake, which was more like a small landing strip. The large, rectangular cake seemed to occupy most of a picnic table. It took me a while to consider the poetry engraved on this confectionery platform. I gazed on the sugar-and-flour delight that represented hours of preparation.

My heart was warmed. A creation like I have never seen before. A family member—no, several women of the Hall family had designed an edible genealogy document, and my family's name was included. I waved David over.

It was a family tree cake. The tree of life that healed all nations. Like Zaccheus, you go up the tree a sinner and come down a saint. No matter where you originated, you are now a Hall. You are flourishing and beautiful. You belong "like a tree planted by a stream." Psalm 1:3

The large tree had a branch representing each sibling in the family, and the leaves had their children's names floating around the branch of their family. Granny Hall was the trunk of the tree, and the clouds in the sky were those who had gone to the great beyond.

The tree was a statement of who you are in the family and who you are in the Kingdom. You knew where you were in the family by your branch level. Your Kingdom placement was heaven (cloud) or earth (tree.)

As I gazed at this "family forest" and tried to memorize all the names of the leaves, Aunt Lydia came up behind me.

"Paula, what do you think of this?" she asked.

The thoughts going through my head were expansive:

1. This is amazing. A cultural collaborative exhibit of art reflecting generational responsibility, resiliency and beauty. And at the same time, a tree that represents the only tree in the garden.

2. It is a theology lesson; it is a generational statement of commitment–it speaks to the fundamental truths of salvation was another unsaid thought.

3. 'I am overwhelmed by the beauty of it all,' might be a better response, because I wanted to be respectful, but I couldn't get the words to come out.

The fullness of my thoughts kept my mouth from moving, so I shook my head and finally mumbled, "It is quite something," as I concentrated on our small leaf.

Aunt Lydia put her arm around me, gave me a little hug and succinctly declared, "There are only two ways to get into this family. Be born into it or lucky enough to marry into it."

I looked at David.

"How did I find such favor with you?"

"At this, she bowed down with her face to the ground. She asked him, "Why have I found such favor in your eyes that you notice me—a foreigner?" Ruth 2:10

Justifying Grace
God's Unmerited Favor Forgiving our Sins

✝

"Justifying Grace implies… a sure trust and confidence that Christ died for 'my' sins, that he loved 'me,' and gave himself for 'me.'" - John Wesley

The Grace of Justification

✝

September 1989

My first week of parenting can be described in one word: complex. My husband David and I were blessed with our first child, Austin. Though I had been excited about his birth, I found that the overwhelming crucible of emotions and bodily changes swept me up in a confusing swirl. Labor, new life, and all the physical transformation in those new days were all-consuming.

During this time, I felt like "a brand *in* the fire." I knew a supernatural force was steadily undergirding me. Plus, I was in the best human company. David could not have been more helpful. But I still felt confused.

Why didn't Austin sleep like the book said he would? What was I doing wrong? I was trying to breastfeed, and I was worn out after intense labor and delivery.

There were ten family members in our 700-square-foot apartment when he was three days old. Austin was the first grandchild on both sides of the family. It was a time to celebrate. God was blessing our family, and I knew it was the most significant moment of my life thus far. Entertaining was my strong suit, but at this time, it was impossible.

I was fractured: one side was exuberant with joy, delighting in the sensations of mothering a child and expressing this with those I loved. Even in the physical challenges, the mental rearrangement of everything, and the life chaos that ensued, my joy was abundant this first week. There had never been a greater sense of being.

Yet many factors made these first weeks very difficult. We were building a home, general contracting it ourselves, hiring all the contractors and project managing the entire thing, and David was working his usual hours. In those days, dads didn't take time off work after their wives had a baby.

We were three weeks from moving into our home when Austin arrived. I planned to go back to work and was preparing for childcare. The first in-home caregiver backed out, and I was at square one. I was trying to walk down many new roads simultaneously; I was tripping up on some and running on others. A new baby, a new home, work–what more could I encounter in this season of life?

Just before we were ready to move into our new home, I had a short afternoon break. I was perched in a crème-colored rocking recliner, a cast-off from Grandma Ruth from the 70s. The recliner had a crushed velvet vibe with dark edges from grubby hands. The baby was sleeping on my lap as I read a few monthly periodicals.

I knew that the two of us must look a bit unfortunate. I was sitting in an apartment over-stuffed with items I was collecting for my new and larger abode. I was a worn-out mother in a garage-sale-worthy chair amid a chaotic room. The dark brown shag rug sadly looked at me, wanting a good vacuum.

Yet the moment was mysteriously transcendent, calling me away from my concerns. Western sunlight coursed through the sliding glass door, showing the dust particles whirling through the late midday air. A slightly jaundiced Austin lay on my lap to absorb the afternoon rays while sleeping. A respite. I relaxed and enjoyed the golden moment.

Picking up the monthly Guideposts magazine, I turned to a story and started to read. It was about a grieving family who had lost a son to bone cancer from a tragic reaction to chemotherapy. I was familiar with the family the story was about; the father was a professor at Butler University and would often come into the science library where I worked during pharmacy school. The article was written by his wife, Judy Osgood. She told about their journey of grief. She shared that during an Easter church service, she made a profound realization: "I knew as never before what God had done for us. I now understood how God felt when His Son, Jesus, died because I, too, had lost a son."

Until then, I had not acknowledged God's amazing sacrifice–for me. Maybe for others, but not for me. I would never have deliberately given up my son. This baby on my lap was to be protected to the death. Even when he was grown, I knew I would safeguard him with no limits. I would not give up my child for anyone, for anything. But God gave up His Son, and it was not an accident. He asked His Son to die for us, including me. It was the epic plan.

At that moment, looking at my newborn son, I realized I had not given myself wholly to the Lord. Through all the years, Jesus was *looking* at me, knowing and *loving* me, but I was *unwilling to acknowledge him*. I did not acknowledge that I was the one who put him on the cross.

The family who lost their baby son chose to trust God's plan, and Jesus was there for them. I realized that Jesus was the most important thing in my life, too. Jesus did not care if I ran the vacuum. My dirty life—me, not the carpet—needed to be cleaned by Warner Sallman's Jesus. At that moment, I knew WSJ. Really knew Him.

The Grace of Faith

✝

"It is the forgiveness of all our sins; and, what is necessarily implied therein, our acceptance with God." - John Wesley, Sermon 'The Scripture Way of Salvation'

Justification by faith is a churchy-church phrase. The doctrine is relatively easy to grasp. Throughout my childhood, I heard many sermons on justification by faith alone. I held that no works were necessary to achieve my salvation. "It is by faith you are saved…" I heard it, but I didn't fully understand it.

It took a magazine article, a quiet afternoon, and the emotions of new motherhood to truly impress on my heart the meaning of Christ's sacrifice.

"The wind blows wherever it pleases. You hear its sound. But you cannot tell where it comes from or where it is going. So it is with everyone born of the Spirit...
"For God so loved the world, that he gave his one and only begotten Son, that whoever believes in him should not perish but have everlasting life..." John 1:8; John 3:16

God often uses many different influences to shape his vessels. For me, a simple tool was used by God to bring revelation. A story written by someone with a random distant connection. In John Wesley fashion, "My heart was strangely warmed."

On February 9, 1709, the parsonage where John Wesley lived with his parents and siblings went up in flames. As their house burned, Wesley's parents, Reverend Samuel Wesley and his wife Susanna, brought their family into the garden. Only then did they discover that their fifteenth and youngest child was still in the house. Wesley was six years old at the time.

By a miracle, he did escape. He became very close to his mother because of this event. Susanna used to speak of Wesley as her "brand plucked from the burning." Wesley kept the memory of his miraculous escape from fire very present in his mind. Throughout his life, he referred to himself as "a brand plucked from the fire."

Just like Wesley was plucked from a literal fire, my heart was plucked from a smoldering crushed velvet chair, glowing in the afternoon sunlight.

The Grace of Rescue

✝

We all need to be plucked from the fire. Although I don't believe hell is a literal fire, it is something that has always scared me. To me, hell is the fear of **being *with* a big, scary person**, **being in a scary *place***, and **being *without* a beloved person.**

As a child, those fears took on faces. The face of **being *with* a big scary person** was Santa Claus. The large man with white beard was a big no-go. I liked Santa from a far distance, but not up close, *alone.*

It was in Mrs. Havey's first-grade classroom that I first found out there was no Santa Claus. I overheard someone telling this startling news to another classmate. I told Mrs. Havey what I heard. She smiled. That's it.

Are you kidding me? This was headline news to me. Breaking News. Put out an APB for Santa–I still believe! A smile was all I got. I was expecting a very sad face with an explanation. Perhaps sympathy? Not even a serious look, as if she was a little disturbed by this news. I was upset.

Mrs. Harvey was scary. She ostracized me in front of the entire class for not putting my name in the correct place on a paper. She scoffed while waving the paper, "Paula put her name on this paper and THEN asked if it was in the correct place!" I was six. I believe this is why I was terrified to ask questions thereafter.

Another time, a classmate wet her pants, and I was very sad for her. I knew she was likely too scared to ask to go to the bathroom. Perhaps the fear of being *with* a big scary person was also in part from my experiences with Mrs. Havey.

Second, I was afraid of **being in a scary *place.*** I was terrified of fun houses at the fair. I once made my younger sister go in front of me because I was too fearful. Who knew what or who was inside those places? Dark and dusty, with corners I could not see into, made me very nervous. I can still see the chipped-painted floors with the black light shining gloomily in the small space. There was a mirror that made objects appear muted and blurry. I ask, where is the "fun" in this? Fun for the person selling the ticket.

Labyrinth mazes still make me queasy to the point of panic. These life-size walking paths feature dead ends and confusion. I get anxious and can't remember the right/left/right as I sweat through my clothing. What if I get forever lost? My loved ones will forget all about me, and I will die in a boxwood entanglement. Or worse–among cornrows.

I was also afraid of **being *without* a beloved person**. I feared my mother would die in the night or that I would get lost in a store.

For me, hell encapsulated all three of these fears. It was fear of being *with* a big scary person and fear of being *without* a beloved person in a scary *place*. In hell, The Most Beloved is absent and the big scary one rules.

Even today, I can't even say "hell" without hesitating. It was a forbidden word in my youth unless it was used in the context of heaven and hell. I still use the name of the Greek god of the underworld, Hades, to refer to the place of burning sulfur.

Why do I struggle with the Biblical concept of hell? Maybe it is because I don't like to see anyone suffer. I cannot enjoy the idea of any human being in hell.

Do I believe that hell is a "lake of fire"? (Rev 20) No, I think it is separation from God. Complete separation from God. What a horrible, horrible thought.

Some would sigh in relief. "Good! No burning in hell. It is JUST a separation from God," says the person on the street.

It is commonplace in our world to say, "War is hell; this disease is hell; the ghetto is hell; go to hell." This is hyperbole.

"Who shall separate us from the love of Christ? Shall tribulation, or distress, or persecution, or famine, or nakedness, or danger, or sword? ...For I am sure that neither death nor life, nor angels nor rulers, nor things present nor things to come, nor powers, nor height nor depth, nor anything else in all creation, will be able to separate us from the love of God in Christ Jesus our Lord." - Romans 8:34,38-39

Hell is a place where not one iota of God's grace penetrates.

I don't care how miserable war or disease, poverty, or how miserable the human condition is--*nowhere are the benefits of God's grace absent.* Where the sun does not shine-where the rain does not fall. Where the air is not to be breathed, that is part of God's grace.

Jesus is the one who talks about the lake of fire and all the ghastly images. I take it symbolically. And the symbol only approximates reality. If it is a location, God does not go near.

That's why we all need Jesus to rescue us, like "a brand plucked from the fire."

The Grace of Salvation

✝

The Valley of Vision

Lord, High and Holy, Meek and Lowly,
Thou hast brought me to the valley of vision,
where I live in the depths but see thee in the heights;
hemmed in by mountains of sin I behold thy glory.

Let me learn by paradox
That the way down is the way up,
That to be low is to be high,
That the broken heart is the healed heart,
That the contrite spirit is the rejoicing spirit,
That the repenting soul is the victorious soul,
That to have nothing is to possess all,
That to bear the cross is to wear the crown,
That to give is to receive,
That the valley is the place of vision.

Lord, in the daytime stars can be seen from deepest wells,
and the deeper the wells the brighter thy stars shine;
Let me find thy light in my darkness,
thy life in my death,
thy joy in my sorrow,
thy grace in my sin,
thy riches in my poverty,
thy glory in my valley.

from _The Valley of Vision,_ a collection of Puritan Prayers

The Grace of Being IN Christ

✝

I am a Christian.
Take out the "A" in Christian – I am a **_Christ In._**

John 17:20-23 CEB I'm not praying only for them but also for those who believe in me because of their word. I pray they will be one, Father, just as you are in me and I am in you. I pray that they also will be in us so that the world will believe that you sent me. I've given
them the glory that you gave me so that they can be one just as we are one. **I'm in them** and you are in me so that they will be made perfectly one. Then the world will know that you sent me and that you have loved them just as you loved me.

Most of the focus when I pray and meditate is on me. My life, my family, my geography. Yet, I want my focus to be on Jesus Christ. It is because of God's great love for his Son that I am included in redemption. From where came this love? Not from anything outside of God himself. God's love comes from himself. Nothing on earth–or in the world—could have merited the love. And there was much (much much) to merit His displeasure. God loved because he wanted to love.

The whole of redemption is a work where we are seen by the Father as belonging to Warner Sallman's Jesus (WSJ). None of us had ever given a Son to him as a sacrifice. And he didn't require it. Instead, he commands us to look to Jesus, who is the Son of God.

The Father gave his **other self,** Jesus. He was the One who visited us and lived with us and inspired Sallman to paint The Gazing Man, Michelangelo to sculpt the marble Pieta, and Da Vinci to depict the dramatic scene of The Last Supper. If there were words to express this love of God, Sallman, Michelangelo, and DaVinci would have made crossword puzzles. Sometimes, art—or an action— speaks louder than any words. And Jesus' action on the cross showed forever just how deeply he loves us.

Romans 5:8: "But God proves His love for us in this: While we were still sinners, Christ died for us." BSB

Sanctifying Grace

God's Unmerited Favor Making Us Holy

"We hold that the wonder of God's acceptance and pardon do not end God's saving work, which continues to nurture our growth in grace.

"Through the power of the Holy Spirit we are enabled to increase in the knowledge and love of God and in love for our neighbor." - John Wesley

The Grace of Timing

1987

The line into the stadium was moving very slowly. It was 1987, and my husband David and I had traveled to New Orleans to watch the Final Four basketball tournament.

The night before, we'd heard some startling news.

"We overbooked, I'm sorry. There are no more rooms available," the hotel clerk had told us.

This was a seriously unfortunate situation for us and for two of David's work colleagues who had traveled to watch the games with us. No room. At the Final Four. What were we going to do? Is this what Mary and Joseph felt like in Bethlehem?

We had traveled a far distance for a planned event. Yet, as we stood amid the throngs of fellow travelers, we realized we were too late. And we were not among the *elite*—which you had to be in order for people to proffer you a room that would be held until you arrived. We were young, like Mary and Joseph, so we searched a little longer.

A couple of hours later, we found a room. The Pinnacle. The name was the opposite of what it offered. Quite like the manger scene, it was a motel that gave us an outdoorsy feel. The door faced a busy highway an hour outside of New Orleans. Yet the bug-infested, dirty-floored, gray-sheeted motel was a place to sleep. Like the Holy couple, we were glad to have it. There were only two rooms available, which meant that Gary and Ralph, the work colleagues (and each a large man), had to sleep in the same room with one double bed. We had a good laugh as we visualized the two of them in the single sagging bed that night—together.

The next morning, we were off to the game.

Our motel set our schedule back considerably for getting to the game. We always liked to get to a game early to walk around the stadium, take in the excitement, and get our snacks before a game. And now we would only arrive just in time.

The line was moving slowly again. The Superdome had at least thirty gates to get in. I chose one. This was back in the day when you had a ticket to punch. I soon realized I'd made the wrong choice.

Why do I always choose the slow line?

Craning my neck to peer ahead, I saw there was a man chatting away at the front.

What?! I can't believe he wants to hold a conversation while 50,000 people are waiting to get in.

"Please, keep the line moving," I gently suggested to the man in front talking to the ticket taker.

He turned.

"Well, hello!" he said with a friendly smile. He laughed.

It was my dad. *Of course.* Dad never missed a chance to strike up a conversation with someone he didn't know.

Now, it was my turn.

"Dad? I didn't know you were coming."

As if anyone behind me in line cared about the logistics of our family at this point.

"Just thought I would come down and watch the games."

"Well, what are the odds that we end up in the same line?" I said, a little annoyed.

He just shrugged.

"Well, I guess we had better let everyone else in," I uttered incredulously.

Oh, and by the way, Indiana won the tournament in a close final game against Syracuse 74-73.

All the delays, all the inconveniences, and yet we had ended up at the right place at the right time to see my dad. A noted grace. A time noted.

I believe God does work behind the scenes–allowing opportunities to draw closer to The Father and sometimes even to your dad.

Time is one device He uses to accomplish his plan. We recognize time as a duration perceived by a shift:

sunrise to sunset, temperatures rise and fall, people age, flowers bloom and fade.

As created beings, time is a tool God uses for transformation. We rarely transform all at once. Instead, we change over time. We are sanctified over time as God works on our hearts. The Creator is not bound by time or space, "For a thousand years in thy sight are but as yesterday when it is past, and as a watch in the night." (Psalm 90:4), but he chooses to use it as an instrument for our renovation and growth.

"In their hearts, humans plan their course, but the LORD established their steps." Proverbs 16:9
God is always working behind the scenes, planning things in advance. He works out the timing perfectly. He works to arrange everything in our lives so that we draw closer to Him.

The Grace of Friendship

Bible Study Fellowship
2003

Rose was a quiet woman. She and I were fellow Bible study students in a church class. She was older than me, yet we had similar study habits. We both enjoyed certain teaching methods.

Rose invited me to a Bible Study outside of our church that was very structured, and I soon became a discussion leader. This experience equipped me with valuable teaching skills. It taught me how to develop a lesson plan and incorporate a variety of materials into my instruction. I learned how to pray with diligence!

Rose and I navigated the study of John together, although we were not in the same discussion group and did not often sit together for lectures. This season of life was bustling: I was in relapse with multiple sclerosis, working as a pharmacist, and my children were young with many school activities. Looking back –why did I say "yes" to her invitation?

During one particularly harrowing interlude during my battle with MS, the prayer chain went out at church. The message asked church members to pray for healing. A short time later, I received an envelope from Rose with a list of eight "healing Scripture passages."

She included instructions: "Read aloud the eight passages from start to finish." She had a sticky note attached that said, "Paula, I love the 2nd one! We will never experience death. We pass from this life to eternal life." (Romans 8:26-28, 34,35a, 38,39)

I read the words aloud. Several times. Which was odd. I wondered, *Why didn't I silently say them to myself?* Life was very busy, and I was exhausted. Did it *really* matter if I recited these verses out loud? I could skim them much faster, but I said them out loud.

And they comforted me.

The standard Bible verses had been used by holy people for centuries, and I had read them as a Christian many times before. They were familiar. However, as I read them aloud, it was as if I were reading them for the first time.

After the John session, I never heard from Rose again. Her husband worked for the post office, and he retired. I heard they moved to central Illinois. They did not leave a forwarding address with the church office. The memory is still kind of "mystical."

Three years later, I went into remission from my MS. And I remain free from MS to this day.

"As you do not know the path of the wind or how the bones are formed in a mother's womb, so you cannot understand the work of God, the Maker of all things." Ecclesiastes 11:15

Rose's Eight Scripture Passages

Matthew 11:28-30
Come to me, all you who are weary and burdened, and I will give you rest. Take my yoke upon you and learn from me, for I am gentle and humble in heart., and you will find rest for your souls. For my yoke is easy and my burden is light.

Romans 8:26-28, 34-35a, 38-39
We do not know what we ought to pray for, but the Spirit himself intercedes for us with groans that words cannot express. And he who searches our hearts knows the mind of the Spirit because the Spirit intercedes for the saints in accordance with God's will. And we know that in all things, God works for the good of those who love him, who have been called according to his purpose. Christ Jesus...is at the right hand of God and is also interceding for us. Who shall separate us from the love of Christ? Neither angels nor demons, neither the present nor the future, nor any powers, neither height nor depth, nor anything else in all creation will be able to separate us from the love of God that is in Christ Jesus our Lord.

Matthew 4:23-24
Jesus went throughout Galilee...healing every disease and sickness among the people. News about him spread...and people brought to him all who were ill with various diseases, those suffering severe pain, the demon-possessed, those having seizures, and the paralyzed, and he healed them.

Matthew 17:20,21
I tell you the truth, if you have faith as small as a mustard seed, you can say to this mountain, 'Move from here to there' and it will move. Nothing will be impossible for you.

John 14:12-14

I tell you the truth, anyone who has faith in me will do what I have been doing. He will do even greater things than these, because I am going to the Father. And I will do whatever you ask in my name, so that the Son may bring glory to the Father. You may ask me for anything in my name, and I will do it.

John 15:5b, 7
Apart from me you can do nothing. If you remain in me and my words remain in you, ask whatever you wish, and it will be given you. This is to my Father's glory…

James 5:15a,16
And the prayer offered in faith will make the sick person well: the Lord will raise him up. If he has sinned, he will be forgiven. Therefore, confess your sins to each other and pray for each other so that you may be healed. The prayer of a righteous man is powerful and effective.

2 Kings 20:5
This is what the Lord, the God of your Father David, says: I have heard your prayer and seen our tears; I will heal you…

Healing Grace

Mulberry, Indiana
1994

When my children were young, I worked in Mulberry, Indiana, an idyllic town similar to Mayberry in the Andy Griffith Show. Mulberry was a few miles east of Lafayette, Indiana and was named after a Mulberry tree that grew where it was founded. It had one tiny main street with a pharmacy where I worked. Main Street also had a taxidermist, a pizza place, *a* pharmacy, and, of course, a church. The street gave way to countryside farmland where the rich black loam made tilling the earth a pleasure. The pharmacy was owned by Tom Holden and his wife, Allison. It had a glass-fronted facade with a door that creaked when you entered. A timeworn table with two high-back wooden benches was placed in front of the opening I peered through while dispensing medicine and counsel. Wooden floors and high ceilings made the small, three-aisle store seem larger than it was.

Every day, coffee was served by Wilma, who was a constant source of historical information about this bucolic town. She let me know who lived where, who was in their family genealogy, and where they worshiped or if they did not worship.

Holden's Pharmacy serviced a nursing home that nestled on the west side of town and provided drug store provisions for the surrounding community. Tom and Allison Holden were both pharmacists and owned two stores. Allison and I mainly split the store hours in Mulberry, and Tom worked the Delphi store. We were small-town "druggists" in the traditional sense.

I worked there for several years, and then my husband and I moved to St. Charles. Shortly after we moved, I found that Tom and Allison Holden were facing a medical crisis. Tom was diagnosed with life-threatening melanoma. The couple prayerfully sought treatment. Tom was turned away by MD Anderson in Houston, Mayo Clinic in Minnesota, and Sloan Kettering in New York.

Rather than offering treatment, the doctors told him, "Get your things in order." Tom and Allison did get their things in order.

After brain surgery, Tom pondered what to do with the cancer hiding in every nook and cranny of his body. Allison found an experimental treatment in Chicago and decided to try this therapy. "Getting things in order" for the Holdens was going to be going for a cure.

Allison and her son, Kirk, stayed with us while Tom received treatment at Lutheran General Hospital in Park Ridge. It was a long journey. It was over two years of treatments, but more than that, there was a sense of anxiety that hung for much longer. God chose to heal him.

Over twenty-five years later, Tom is still the small-town pharmacist everyone loves. He has his own store in Frankfort, Indiana, and Allison is the Teaching Leader for one of the largest Bible Study Fellowships (BSF) Bible Studies.

There are miracles today. No one can predict these works of God. No one can call them up for their pleasure. Ordinary people. Extraordinary circumstances.

Grace given, grace received.

"…but this happened so that the works of God might be displayed in him. As long as it is day, we must do the works of him who sent me…" John 9:3b,4a

Neglected Grace

✝

Often, I overlook the small things, the quiet blessings. In our Bible study, there was another Paula. A quiet Paula. I did not know her well. She was humble, soft-spoken, and cared for her mother. Same-Name Quiet Paula would be labeled a quiet influencer today. She was an introvert. Her strategy was to think first and talk later. This low-key writer was not a talker, and she valued privacy, but her prayers were profound.

Lord God, my Savior, there aren't words to describe how thankful I am for Your many blessings. I pray that You forgive my many sins and give me the knowledge, strength, and courage to live life as You desire us to live. Help me to be worthy of the countless blessings You provide in my life every day. Amen. November 7, 2011

A Prayer by Deborah-by-the Palm Evening class member
Paula Dettman
(July 2, 1955-April 30, 2013)

Quiet Paula has been lifted from this earthly life. It's too late to get to know her. Too late to dash off a letter. Too late to thank her for the subtle, parsed words spoken in class that came so gently. I was able to encourage her in the weekly readings. A nod and smile toward her would be enough in class for her to share unassuming contemplations on the week's assignments. Too late to get more of her impressions. Cancer, in its usual brutal form, took her early from our circle.

How often I neglect people — it is unreasonable!—like the summer rain and God's graces are poured out on me, people swirl around me, and I tromp through the path of life without looking sideways. In psychology, it is called perceptual blindness when you fail to notice something in plain view. It was discovered in the 1970s but first introduced as a concept in 1992 by Irvin Rock and Ariel Mack. In the worst-case scenario, consequences of perceptual blindness in the real world may include auto collisions and successful pick-picketers. Lesser consequences may be a repeated word found by a book editor. My ability to focus attention enables me to ignore irrelevant or distracting information but has led me occasionally to miss something or someone I might have wanted to experience.

My mother gave me an inside-out lesson at a Mother's Day banquet in the 1970s.
My mother and two daughters were in their full glory as we glided into church, all dressed up, for an evening socializing with friends for the annual Mother's Day Banquet.
All the ladies of the church assembled, even if they didn't have a daughter. After all, everyone *was* a daughter. People brought their guests—a mother from afar, a sister who lived in a neighboring town, or even a daughter-in-law from the nearby Baptist church. There was food and a program.
The food was delicious and plenteous: ham and bacon-infused in the casseroles, Jell-O salads with layers, creations encased in glass trifle bowls, crisp lettuce lined the vegetable trays, and the ever-present deviled eggs.
In this era, there was nothing made from a box or store-bought. All selections were worthy of praise and personal identification.
Each table was adorned with a tablecloth and a centerpiece. There were paper doilies on plates, and ladies brought their best glassware. My mother's lime Jell-O with cottage cheese and pineapple had been nestled in a unique mold that made it tasty and beautiful. I have the copper mold today.
The program consisted of music and lovely poems about mothers. Proverbs 31 was recited, and everyone received a flower of some sort. There were presentations for United Methodist Women who had served that year in particular ways or had been members for an extended time.
It was a lovely evening—unless you were a teenager.
At this particular Mother's Day Banquet, we came into the church. I exchanged perfunctory niceties with others and sat down at one of the tables. The usual crowd was there: the minister's wife and numerous others. The basement was filling up, and I was biding my time.
I looked around and thought, "OK, two hours tops, and we will be done."
The minister's wife, Mrs. Bastain, was sitting at another table. Mother went over to talk with her. *Chat chat chat.* She came back to our table, and I knew something was up.

"Paula, since Mrs. Bastain doesn't have a daughter, I told her you would sit with her this evening!" my mother said with a smile.

The evening suddenly went from, "ho-hum, I can tolerate" to "I have been thrown into the furnace!" Two hours of small talk with the minister's wife seemed like a Shadrach, Meshach, Abednego state of emergency. I glanced at my mother (A.K.A Nebuchadnezzar) for a last-minute reprieve. A look only known between mother and daughters made my fate known. I could feel my face burning. My head was swirling. I had to get control. The furnace was heating up. Why not my younger sister Amy? She is cute–she could even be adorable at times. Likely, Mom knew Amy would have cried or pouted and not had the social skills to endure the event with this woman.

Mrs. Bastain had taught our confirmation class—God Bless her. What I remember of this class is learning the creeds, commandments, and graces and knowing that Warner Salman's Jesus was in the same room.

That aside, this was a fire I had to fight in about two seconds or less. I had no time to react. I knew if I showed any emotion, Mother would be disappointed, as would *Jesus*. He could see every move. Mrs. Bastain smiled—just like my mother was smiling.

Sallman's Jesus was ever restrained. No empathy. *Just do it.* What was I waiting for? Move over to Mrs. Bastain's table.

Into this fiery furnace of dullness (I thought) I went. I left the table with my mom, sister, and friends and went to Mrs. Bastain's table, which was filled with older women. They were perfectly lovely women—however, the gap of unfamiliarity was infinite. Together, we enjoyed the program. I smiled at Mom, and her face became more empathetic as the night went on.

My mother and Jesus had a plan at the Mother's Day banquet and executed it together. Mrs. Bastain had a "daughter" to sit with. I would have never remembered the Mother's Day Banquet unless Mom threw me into the furnace that night. Some lessons require heat. I am thankful that I was thrown in that evening. I don't recall any banquets with clarity before or after.

✝✝✝

Many times, I don't voluntarily choose to reach out. I neglected Quiet Paula. I pass by lonely, quiet people. As a result, I miss out on the joy that God is sending me in the form of quiet, lonely people.

Who have I overlooked in a hurry, hurry, hurry? Or perhaps I neglected someone because I didn't even know **how** to have a relationship with them. Or because I thought it was too hard. I reasoned that I didn't have enough room in my life.

The chances I have overlooked, when I have been too intimidated to take action or if I constantly, faithlessly discard situation after situation, moment after moment, as insignificant, I have simply had no place to display God's kingdom grace.

God comes before our minds through small, quiet, individual experiences. Selfishness says, "I don't want my own experience violated, or my own plans messed up." Consequence: I don't see his Grace.

I can neglect His grace, but it is not wasted. God's gift does not change or diminish. Only by abiding in Christ and submitting to the pruning knife of God (sometimes in the form of a mother at the annual Mother's Day Banquet where a fiery furnace is used) as he cuts away all that is unimportant in order to remain wholeheartedly in Christ is when grace can be experienced.

Abiding in Christ: allowing His Word to fill our minds, direct our wills, and transform our affections.

The Grace of Fellowship

Deborah by The Palm Beginnings
2006

*"Deborah, a prophetess, with the wife of Lappidoth, was leading Israel at that time. She held court under **the Palm of Deborah** between Ramah and Bethel in the hill country of Ephraim, and Israelites came to her to have their disputes decided." -Judges 4:4-5*

Deborah-by-the-Palm Bible Study began as a small group of United Methodist Women who yearned for a greater understanding of the Bible. We knew that God had created us with a basic human need for close personal relationships. Learning Bible facts will make little difference in a person's life, but learning the epic story of God in the context of relationships can transform people.

Charles and John Wesley held group meetings at Oxford, which were known as the "Holy Club" because they spent their afternoons praying, studying Scripture, and taking Communion. This was a scornful name for the band of brothers that assembled. But we wanted to imitate their great example. Our new Bible study gained a reputation for being the "hard" Bible Study because it required homework, essays, and attendance. We declared a purpose: "...to create in each participant a personal relationship with God--to Love God-- through daily Bible study and apply knowledge to daily life... to be filled with spiritual wisdom and understanding so as to walk in a manner pleasing to the Lord, bearing fruit in every good work."

The group's name came from the prophetess Deborah. A few women formed the group from an already-existing United Methodist Women's circle named "Deborah." I did not want to confuse meeting times in church communications, so I simply added "by the Palm" to the name. That is where I pictured Deborah judging in the desert: by the palm.

Deborah was the noble prophetess, warrior, and respected leader of Israel. This woman made crucial decisions for the people of Israel. She helped form opinions on business transactions, moral issues, and more. She facilitated negotiations, mediated, and provided direction and encouragement.

There is no record of anyone disputing her decisions because she was a woman. Perhaps that is how I envisioned our members: we would grow into women of strength and influence through reading our Bibles gathered together by our imaginary palm tree.

The palm tree vision seems ridiculous now, but perhaps it has a basis in Scripture, after all. Trees have been a visual from the beginning of the Bible. In Genesis 1 and 2, the trees are said to be fruitful and pleasing to the eye. There are trees or a component of a tree in every covenant story. The first Psalm says the blessed, righteous one will flourish like a tree planted by a stream. Jesus dies on a tree for everyone. The last story of the Bible depicts the Tree of Life that heals every nation. The decision was made: "Deborah *by the* Palm" was perfect: DB P.

However, what we got was less than desirable palm-tree, oasis-laden surroundings. Our group would get annexed to the lower level musty and cold narthex, where I had to supplement with my leftover lamps brought from home and an air freshener. I needed a breeze from a palm tree.

At times, we would be in the parlor or fellowship hall, wherever the Rotary or Book Club was not meeting that week. There were no Palm trees within a thousand miles, but it didn't dampen the attendance. The Spirit undergirded His work. Scripture was amplified as we read. Our fellowship magnified the beauty of the Word and diminished the harsh surroundings.

The spirit of Deborah, the mighty prophetess, was among us. Her courage, confidence, wisdom, and trust in the Lord ran through our weekly meetings.

The Grace of Unity

✝

Deborah-by-the Palm Women's Bible Study

Young moms, older moms, grandmothers, and others would navigate their way into Deborah-by-the Palm from various places. To be a member of the study group, you had to be... Come to think of it, I suppose there were no requirements. Come as you are. New

Christian, old Christian, need-to-be-renewed Christian, on-the-fence Christian, rock-solid Christian, and not a Christian.

Somebody would invite somebody else. Those somebodies became acquaintances who became friends.

The somebodies joined together to become a mosaic. Seen from a distance, a mosaic is a single entity of glistening beauty. Up close, each unique individual tesserae or pebble tile is intricately layered together in various patterns. The fragments that became the mosaic allowed for a common vision and provided space for our differences. Christ was the unifying thread, something greater than friendship that ran through that hour together.

Our nucleus consisted of seven women seven "fragments" that formed the center of the mosaic. Each was brought into the circle by a Radial Force. Like a lasso twirling, the little group was drawn towards the center as if by a mysterious force. *The* Force. Each divinely unique, all seeking a Center.

Carol: She must be a lost cousin of Joseph, Jacob's son. Carol always sees the positive in situations. She is faithful, forgiving, and helps the group return to loving thoughts. Thank you for this trait!

Kristin: Always prepared and diligent in her homework. Kristin is a great worker inside and outside the church.

I admire her gift of music and how organized she is.

Sharon K: She used to be the quiet one! Now, she is always contributing her thoughts and understanding.

There has been growth with Sharon. Her witness has been influential upon me and others.

Michele: Still, waters run deep. Michele will be private and then say something so profound. Absolutely profound. There is much depth with Michele, who is an anchor to our class.

Laura: A Southern girl with a large heart, her gift of hospitality and joy expressed through family love is contagious.

Sharon W.: Sharon knows when you need "God with skin." Sharon sends a card for every birthday and anniversary and will drop off a bag of chocolates at your home at just the moment needed--or right before.

Over time, I watched these unique individuals knit together through weekly one-hour Bible study and sharing of personal lives. The women became a close-knit group of eclectic souls. Holy Club. A suitable name for those seeking that which is Holy.

One day after Bible study, six women rushed away from church on a sunny fall day. We grabbed You-Pick-Twos at Panera and gathered around a table. The restaurant was still crowded at 12:30, but the hubbub simmered down by 1:30. The group talked late about the fringes, hollows, and fullness of life we had embraced and how we had changed. As the tides rise and fall, we would be there next week, but the conversation would be different—not personally intimate. Small talk does fall short of meaningful conversation, and if it never crosses over to substantive, the relationships can become empty. We were still there at 2:00… and 3:00. There was a beauty I had never witnessed. Words were spoken kindly, softly. Laughter came easily. No great theology was spoken, but the conversation was thoughtful, and we spoke of the meanderings of life: heart to heart. We spoke to one another to be heard. The narrative of our lives. The westward windows filtered the autumn afternoon sun rays into the room, shimmering into the spangled dust hanging in the air. There was a sacred presence around us, a heavenly place where the Father held his love. That Heavenly Place was revealed around this table. The mystery of this afternoon was a secret hiding place. No loud trumpets declaring the presence of God, patrons of the restaurant only smiled at our laughter going unnoticed otherwise.

Later, I asked a participant in this circle, and she did not recall the breath of paradise in our words or setting. I realized that God's Light had been touching me and filling my heart personally. The food was not our meal that day. It was not limited by language or words. I was taken prisoner by the Spirit, my body was warmed, and the heavenlies were made visible to my soul. The words spoken on earth were sent from above. I was given a sense of contentment by this circle and flow of conversation.

As each of us shared time and words, the Spirit infused us together with joy, love, and heavenly illumination. Our fellowship was greater than the sum of its parts: more than the simple words, the simple people, and the simple food we shared. We were a mosaic of beauty and light.

The Grace of God's Word—Sweeter than Honey

Deborah by the Palm Bible Study

Psalm 19:9-10 "The decrees of the Lord are firm, and all of them are righteous. They are more precious than gold, than much pure gold; they are sweeter than honey, than honey from the honeycomb." NIV

Over the Fourth of July weekend, my daughter's future husband, Brandon, was helping David in our yard. They were staking the hydrangeas. The hydrangeas were giant Annabelles, and the garden framed our front entrance. The blooms could be cut and dried in the fall to make gorgeous winter bouquets.

Staking the hydrangeas was an annual activity. It was David's favorite garden project because the large blooms showcased our home when they stood tall. It was a must-do project.

As the two men were working together, Brandon noticed bees swarming overhead. David thought his future son-in-law was trying to divert attention from the gardening so he could speed up the outing to the golf course that David had promised later in the day. But Brandon persisted in swatting the bees. Brandon is 6'8" and was getting the high-altitude bees a little more than David. Finally, David saw that there really were bees—a lot of them. They were coming in and out of our vent above our garage. Our neighbor Paul, seeing the ruckus, strolled across the street, and another neighbor, Eric, also joined in the bee fest. Paul, who had a beehive in his backyard, identified them as honeybees. Hearing this, the men discarded the bee spray and decided to investigate a little more. After prodding and poking—yes, we drilled large and small holes in several places of the wall. Following the emanating buzzing sound, we found a hive deep between the wall of the garage and the room above the garage. It was very large—imagine a 75-inch television, but instead, this is a honeycomb inside your walls. After drilling and searching, we were glad to have hit "gold" but shocked at our find. Honey: Great! Bees: What do we do?

Our neighbor Paul gave us the name of a professional beekeeper who specialized in extracting bees. Over the next week, he found over 50,000 bees in the wall of our home. He built a large scaffolding in front of our house and commenced the delicate operation of finding the queen. The quest for the bees became quite a spectacle, providing entertainment for passersby. It took a while, over a week, but the beekeeper eventually found the queen bee. Neighbors and friends shared in our amusement with the bees.

Over the next few weeks, the professional beekeeper extracted sixty pounds of honey! The honeycomb that came from this hive was unbelievably good. The beekeeper brought the bucket down with a sampling of honeycomb for us to taste, and David and I were like bears pawing for the next bite.

This event provided a signpost that pointed me toward the study material I would use in Deborah by the Palm Bible Study that year. I found a guidebook written by a local woman, and she gave me permission to copy her book for our use. I was thrilled. Guess what its name was? It was called *Honey for the Heart: A Meditative Study of Psalms* by Mary Jane Young!

The bee became our symbol for Bible Study that year.

We realized that in Jewish gematria (number study), that year was the year of the Bee! Again, God was working everything together for good, in his perfect timing and in his perfect way. We became friends with Pete, the beekeeper, and he said we had a lifetime supply of honey. And God continued to supply us with the sweet nourishment of his word, in lifetime supply. Sweeter than honey.

Psalm 119:103: "How sweet are your words to my taste, sweeter than honey to my mouth!" NIV

Grace in the White Space

Deborah by the Palm Bible Study
2015

In 2015, Deborah by the Palm Bible Study began the year traveling with the apostle Paul. We read a historical fiction book, <u>Apostle Paul: A Novel,</u> by James Cannon. It was an epic drama of Paul, and the class loved this book. The author's sensitive portrayal of the apostle as human and earthy, along with Paul's scholarly side, mixed with his passion for life, helped bring the stories alive.

"I don't think I would have liked this apostle, Paul," exclaimed Carol G. "He is too... just too..." She couldn't find the word to finish her sentence. Crowded in Mrs. Grayson's white space were contemplations of who the letter-writer was. And it was disagreeable, even abrasive. "And there occurred such a sharp disagreement that they separated from one another, and Barnabas took Mark with him and sailed away to Cyprus." Acts 15:38

Mrs. Grayson wrestled with this. The entire class contemplated the apostle's boldness and debated whether or not they would have been offended by his manner as it is depicted in Scripture—and historical fiction.

Faithful to the course, Carol G. came to know the apostle better. She remained a bit aggravated with Paul but continued to read with dedication.

I reminded the class that this book was historical *fiction*. Although it was a historical context for our future study of Acts and Philippians, it was not a factual account of what Paul did.

I then reconsidered my rebuke. I realized there are many gaps in the biblical texts that allow for the reader's pondering, meditation, and consideration.

Generations of life fit in the white spaces. The Truth remains, but the white spaces may be filled in. We live in the white space. Author James Cannon filled out white spaces, and the class loved it. It was Cannon's white space. And it got them to think about how they would fill their own white spaces, the gaps between the words.

Grace to Magnify God

Deborah by the Palm Bible Study—Book of Luke
2011-2012

Essay-writing set our class apart from others. In order to digest our topics more deeply, we wrote essays to share our thoughts with the rest of the class.

I wanted each student to embrace more of their own story intertwined with a Biblical prompt or not-so-Biblical prompt. After startled looks and maybe some "goading" by this Bible study teacher, I had many participants. Science tells us that when we hear a story, our bodies produce oxytocin and form a connection with the person we are listening to. Stories bind us together and help us make sense of our experiences. Oxytocin induces antistress effects, such as reducing blood pressure and cortisol levels and promoting healing. Sharing and cultivating our thoughts is an act of vulnerability and it forms our identity within our community. Essay day was a lazy river in a world that was serving up turbulence. We could laugh together, cry at loves lost, ponder the mysteries of Heaven, and be wide-eyed with personal perceptions.

The community of believers has been built on stories. We are a people made for relationships– with our Creator and one another. These essays are more than an answer to a prompt, they allow us to trace our past and shape the footsteps of our future.

Each essay is relevant and vital and helps form the unending circle of fellowship required for a vibrant faith life.

This simple book started…one word at a time, one essay at a time. Try it.

When we studied the book of Luke, I assigned essays on the topic of "How Do I Magnify God?" based on Mary's prayer in Luke 1:46-49: "And Mary said: 'My soul **glorifies the Lord**, and my spirit rejoices in God my Savior, for he has been mindful of the humble state of his servant. From now on, all generations will call me blessed, for the Mighty One has done great things for me—holy is his name.'"

How Do I Magnify GOD?
By Michele Claney
2011

This question makes me uncomfortable. It is my *intention* to model Christian behavior, share my talents and try to push beyond my comfort zone to magnify God. However, to answer this question is to also think about where I do *not* magnify God. I read a quote that says, "We magnify or shrink God in what we say and do." That kind of sums up my thoughts after mulling over this question. I can give a list of things that I did that I think magnify God. For me, the reality is that the bigger I can make God in my life the more I will magnify him.

"We magnify or shrink God in what we say and do. It is not as though we make God bigger; but we come to grips with how big God is. We magnify God if what God says is what we do; but we shrink God if we only 'talk the talk and don't 'walk the walk.' We shrink God if our work does not match our worship. Easy here, on Sunday morning, to sing the songs of Advent and to feel the joy of being together in God's presence; harder to go out and put God's presence into practice. Mary not only magnified God in her singing but more so magnified God by putting her own body on the line." –Dr. Gareth W. Icenogle

✝✝✝

How Do I Glorify God?
By Joni DeDobbelaere
2011

Wow, that's a hard question. As I have pondered this question the last few weeks, I can think of many BIG ways in
which my friends and family glorify the Lord, but for me…I am stuck.
I **don't** chair fundraisers for the needy.
I **don't** teach bible study classes.
I **don't** take middle schoolers away for a week to be with God.

Those things are just not me. Then it hit me. For me, it's all about the little things that I do that glorify God.

I **do** teach my children how to pray.
I **do** respect my husband and follow the commandments of the Lord.
I **do** give freely of my time and resources to help others.

And I **do** love the Lord with all my heart, soul, and mind.

Glorifying God
By Kathy Kozak
2011

I like to think that I glorify God by simple acts of kindness. An example would be cleaning my 84-year-old mother's bathroom. She might not even be aware of my deed, and certainly would not know that I spent 45 minutes taking extra care so that it is cleaner than it needs to be. I feel that the urge to do this is a reflection of God's love that he demonstrated through Jesus dying on the cross. The degree of love and compassion His act demonstrated set an example that it is easy to get to a game early—to walk around the stadium, take in the excitement, and get our snacks before a game. And now we could only arrive just in time.

✝✝✝

How do I Glorify God?
By Mary Linebarger

This is a tough essay!

It is almost as tough for me to write as it is for me to actually get through a day without letting the Lord down.

When I found out I had cancer, it was quite a shock. I was scared, angry, scared, worried about things that were to come, scared, worried about things that wouldn't get done, scared, worried about my animals, and then just plain scared!

I asked God to please help me through this, to please give me strength, and most of all, PLEASE don't let it hurt!!!! Within the next couple of days, or maybe it was the next morning, I can't remember; I received a peace of mind that I can't describe. All my worries were gone! I had accepted my fate, whatever that might be. I could block fear out of my mind and just go on as if nothing had happened.

Every day, I get up and try to glorify God by being the best that I can be. I try to be a light in this world for God by being happy and helpful. Trying to be positive in people's lives and bring others joy. I feel that I need to show people that God is with me every minute of the day. I consider this part of my life's journey but always seem to fall down on the path sometime during the day.

I WANT TO SHOW PEOPLE THAT THE DEVIL CAN TAKE EVERYTHING I HAVE, BUT HE CAN'T TAKE MY JOY… The problem is that this has become a battle between me and the devil. He seems to come creeping around every day, whispering all the negative thoughts in my head until I EXPLODE at someone or have some mean, evil, nasty comment come out of my mouth at a poor, unsuspecting stranger.

I WOULD LOVE TO GLORIFY GOD BY TELLING EVERYONE I KNOW THAT:
GOD IS REAL

GOD IS THERE
GOD IS MY TEACHER, COMFORTER, HEALER
AND I FEEL BLESSED TO HAVE GONE THROUGH THESE LAST 6 YEARS BECAUSE I FEEL THAT I KNOW
GOD IS BETTER THAN I EVER WOULD HAVE.
I am still knocking the devil off my shoulder every day, and one day, I will get rid of him and be able to make it through.
The day without letting my Lord down.
PRAISE GOD!!!!!!!!!!!!!!!
You know, he just never lets up…The devil is telling me that he is stupid and should start over!

✝✝✝

1 Corinthians 10:31
"…or whatever you do, do it for the glory of God."

Grace for Humility

Deborah by the Palm Bible Study—Book of Isaiah
2011

"These are the ones I look on with favor:
those who are humble and contrite in spirit,
and who tremble at my word." Isaiah 66:2b

Essay Prompt:
"Describe an embarrassing or humbling moment."

The day we shared these essays, there was laughter and tears. Sharing our vulnerabilities strengthened our bonds. Even our truly humbled moments, when shared, can bring true love of friendship to heal the memory.
God loves us in all our moments. Whether we are big or small, prideful or humble, God gives us opportunities to teach us.

Be Careful What You Say
By Tina Gagner

One embarrassing experience came when my daughter Erin was about 7 years old. We had been living in our neighborhood for about 3 years. During that time, we had met and conversed with all of the neighbors around us except two. They were a younger couple that lived across the street. They were hardly ever around. When you did see them, they never waved or made eye contact. Their cars would come home, go into the garage, and we'd never see them again. My husband and I jokingly said they were in the Witness Protection Program and referred to them as "The Witness Protection People."

A conversation at our house between my husband and me would go something like this:
Me: "Did you see they cut down that tree?"
Phil: "Which tree?'
Me: "You know, the one in front of the neighbor's house."
Phil: "Which neighbor?"
Me: "The Witness Protection People"
Phil: "Oh, that tree."

Then, one day, while I was up in the bathroom, Erin answered our front door. I yell down, asking who it is. She says something inaudible, so I ask again. I hear her the second time loud and clear.

"THE WITNESS PROTECTION LADY."

Much to my embarrassment, not only has Erin repeated something that was meant to remain between my husband and me, but the neighbor is also standing right there with the door open! Turns out she needed a ride somewhere, during which I learned that she and her husband worked long hours and traveled a lot, and she regretted that they didn't socialize with the neighbors more.
Boy, did I ever feel bad?

✝✝✝

Spiritually Humbled by God
By Sharon Krusinski

What is humility? It is the condition of being humble. Humble is defined as showing awareness of one's shortcomings. Humility is not bitter anger; it sees the mercy of God. Pride sees only the pain. As some of you know, my daughter Leah has been diagnosed with occipital neuralgia, which is nerve pain in the back of her head. It is a pain that never goes away, but the intensity of the pain just changes. When this started about a year and a half ago, I never thought she would still be dealing with it now. We aren't any closer to finding a solution to the problem than we were in the beginning. It is so discouraging and frustrating as a mother not to be able to make your child feel better. I have done a lot of praying about this situation. I have asked you to please show me some way to help her. I have taken her to general doctors, neurologists, physical therapists, chiropractors, and massage therapists. She has tried different medications. She has had MRIs, CAT scans, and EEGs. Nothing has helped. I know God doesn't always answer the way or when we want, but I haven't been able to understand why it has to go on like this. Why can't she feel better? It made me begin to question everything. Am I not listening? Am I not praying hard enough or the right way? Am I doing things wrong in my life?

A couple of weeks ago, I told Paula that I was going to stop coming to Bible Study. I have been so frustrated and discouraged. Nothing had changed for Leah, so I found myself shutting everyone out. I didn't want to talk about it to anyone. I just wanted to be alone with my thoughts. After I had decided to quit, I thought I would feel a huge sense of relief. I expected to feel really good about my decision. I didn't. I felt more conflicted than ever.

Then came this essay and Isaiah 40. I felt a real comfort after reading the 40th chapter. I also researched pride and humility on the internet, and it relates to pain. I learned that with pride, we want to have the last word, but with humility, God has the final say. Pain can either reduce us to humility or elevate us to pride. I was allowing Leah's pain to take me away from God. Pride was winning. I am now able to see that. Humility can help me have a better connection with God. It's just up to me to decide who or what can help me do that.

1 Peter 5:6-7 says, "So humble yourselves under the mighty power of God, and at the right time he will lift you up in honor. Give all our worries and cares to God, for he cares about you."

Leah is a trooper; she has her bad day, but she continues on the best she can. I will continue to ask God to be with her and guide her through the difficult times. I hope and pray that, in time, her pain will go away.

Postscript: Leah is now a nurse and happily married, and the headaches are gone. Sharon was a reluctant essay writer. It was worth the wait.

"Comfort, comfort my people,
says your God...Every valley shall be raised up,
every mountain and hill made low;
the rough ground shall become level..." Isaiah 40:1,4

My Most Embarrassing Moment
By Marge Meanger

Note: Marge was approximately 75 years old at the time of writing this essay

My most embarrassing moment occurred when I was a teenager. I had attended a pajama party and did not get much if any, sleep. Four of us had planned to attend the morning church service and missed breakfast. The day turned out to be much hotter than predicted. As the service progressed, I started feeling a little weird. The heat was getting to me because I was overdressed. The air was overwhelmingly hot, and I was starving and hungry. My ears felt like they were filling with water.

Before I knew what happened, I fainted, and I was sitting outside in the fresh air on the church bench. An usher and a few people gathered around as I came to. I was so embarrassed to learn that I had fainted, and an usher had carried me out of the pew for some fresh air.

My greatest concern had been whether or not my skirt had stayed down. I will never know the answer to that embarrassing question.

Grace for the Mundane

Deborah by the Palm Bible Study
2009

Hair ye, Hair ye

I have asked DB✝P class members to write responses on many topics over the years. Yet the topic that elicited the most heartfelt response was a unique one: "Hair."
I thought it would be a fun topic. I did not know it would be an emotional rollercoaster ride. The prompt was simple: "Write about hair–your hair." I had to explain it wasn't a religious statement. Just hair.
I will only include a few of the essays:
I'll start with my own.

✝✝✝

Hair

October 28, 2009
By Paula Hall

I think about my hair too much. I want thick, shiny, manageable hair that I can blow-dry into tresses around my face or pull back into a swelling pony-tail. Of course, the color should be a glowing brown with streaks of natural blonde flowing through it…in only a few spots.
What do I have? Thin, fine hair that is the color of January mud. Thank goodness for hair products, blow-dryers, highlights, and a good hairdresser. With the help of these, I achieve a "color-of-the-month flyaway hair-sprayed, teased, disheveled look that is ho-hum at best. Every day, I look in the mirror and fiddle, spray, brush, and visualize other people's hair that I want to imitate. Maybe a "Meg Ryan" or "Meg Bingham" look today!

Yes, I covet other women's hair in my close circle of friends…a.k.a. Bible study ladies. Is this a sin? Or is it admiration that I want to improve myself through hair therapy? Michele has wispy hair that looks terrific with her winsome party sweater, Ann comes in with her sophisticated pulled-back ponytail, while Carol has the famous "Muffy" as her hairdresser that we all know and love. We have new members that have long, luscious hair… Kristine, Linda, Tamara, Bridget, ugh, it would take until I was 80 to get her long hair, and then it would be tangled and fried. Hillary has a cute short cut that frames her face perfectly, and Gina and Kathy have curls galore. Do you see my problem? I cannot concentrate on teaching my class due to my hair haplessness.

I want what I cannot have. God has given me "this thorn in my side" –mealy hair. Every woman wants Clairol Girl hair, and I must remember, "his grace is enough."

The women of the bible who were noted for their beauty must have had hair that was out-of-the-ordinary. Esther was "lovely to look at,' and this had to give her the edge in her quest for the king's attention. I don't think she had a bad hair day when she approached king Xerxes with her request. "Jacob loved Rachel more than Leah." I bet Rachel had better hair. Maybe a better braid or something. They always go back to the line about Leah's eyes…I don't think so; it was the hair. Deborah, our beloved name's sake, had to command many men, and I do not believe that she could have done this with messy hair in the desert. She had to have manageable hair in a bun put under her scarf in a business-like fashion to be authoritative.

I must settle for my mop top and know it is God's will. It keeps me humble. What if I had the beautiful hair I dreamed of? It would create problems of pride. I will keep the sin of coveting!

✝✝✝
Much 'Do About Hair
October 28, 2009
Kathryn M. Kozak

Thinking about the significance of hair in my life brings forth so many thoughts and emotions that it makes my head spin. I first think of how I got stuck with my father's thin mouse-brown hair while my two sisters inherited my mother's thick, luxurious coif.

I next recall a traumatic experience I had in the third grade. For some mysterious reason, I granted my older sister permission to cut my hair. Unfortunately, the result was a much shorter-than-expected hack job. This was so traumatic to my delicate, formative self that I insisted on covering my hair on the lengthy walk to school. This was a bad choice because it involved wearing a hooded raincoat while walking in 90-degree weather. I still remember feeling the embarrassment of the bad cut, which outweighed the weirdness of being the only kid wearing a stifling raincoat in hot weather. I ask myself, "Why was this so important to me?"

I think that in our society, hair status and self-esteem are so closely connected that a perceived bad hairdo can ruin even a third-grader's day. We all grow up with images of Rapunzel letting her hair down and Clairol's beautiful girls' exotic tresses waving at us in their commercials. Surely, we are taught that beauty and self-worth are connected, and hair is a big part of this…

...One last thought examines the different approaches to hair and aging between the sexes. It seems unfair that the salt and pepper look is often perceived as a sign of experience and maturity with men, but for ladies, gray hair tends to suggest that they are losing their status and credibility.

Why is it that a woman's vitality appears to be more closely tied to her hair color than that of a man? All of us know that graying hair has nothing to do with what we are capable of. Men, of course, are not immune to the threat of gray hair and its influence on how they are perceived. For example, my fellow coworker, "Al", has a bald head with a standard ring of hair that mysteriously began to slowly change from grey to brown over approximately one year. This man excels in projecting self-confidence, yet many of us suspect there is a chink in his self-esteem somewhere. This placates us in light of the tiresome superiority complex he frequently portrays. In the final analysis, it seems that hair is a fascinating topic that covers many aspects of humanity—social and economic indicators, teenage rebellion, self-expression, and health status, to name a few. I just have to try to stop coveting all of the great hair that comes my way!

Postscript: Kathy and I have had many conversations on hair. We live next door to one another. We have lamented our lack of full-bodied hair, pondered the genetic code given to our scalps, and spoken covetous words over those with lovely locks while sitting by the fireplace.

✝✝✝

Bad Hair Days

By Sharon Krusinski

When Paula said that we were going to write an essay about hair, my first thought was that she was crazy. I didn't really think that I had any stories about my hair. The next day, I started thinking about it. I began to think of so many things that I had to make a list.

I realized that I have so many vivid memories of things that had happened to my hair. For example, the first time I had my hair cut short (probably third grade), I yelled at the hairdresser and told her that I hated it. My mom made me go back later to apologize. I got perms from my mom at different times while I was growing up. When I look back at those pictures, I am in shock. What was my mom thinking? It looked awful. One of the last hair disasters was probably about 16 years ago. My sister-in-law said she would highlight my hair for me. I figured that would be fine since she did my mother-in-law's hair. Well ... my hair was bright orange in the back. I'm sure my husband remembers being in our basement (he didn't want anyone seeing him through the window), putting more hair dye on for me, and trying to get it back to its normal color. It didn't work. I ended up at the hair salon getting it fixed. Thank goodness the hairdresser knew what she was doing. After that experience *only* hairdressers could touch my hair.

I don't know why hair is so important. I guess it is a big part of our image. I always worry if the color is right; if it is too long or too short, should I get a different style. I'm not the only one who worries about their hair. My daughter wants lighter hair, my son gets his hair cut exactly every 4 weeks and my husband, who unfortunately has lost a little of his hair, wants more hair. We never seem happy.

It's a coincidence that Paula asked us to write this essay at a time when my hairdresser is going through chemo for breast cancer. Christina is a very pretty Italian girl, 29 years old. She had beautiful, long, dark, curly hair. After her first treatment, it started coming out in clumps. She finally shaved it and now has no hair at all. I fight with my hair every day, wanting it to be just right. When I think of Christina, it makes me think twice about worrying about it. My son told me that Christina said that her biggest worry now is whether she should put on her wig or go out and get the mail. That puts what is important into perspective for me. Maybe the essay wasn't a coincidence after all.

✝✝✝

Ode to the Animal Lover
By Mary Linebarger

Hair here, hair there
Hair is almost everywhere

Hair on the dog
Hair on the frog
Hair on the floor
Hair on the door

Hair on the stair
Hair in the air
It's all over, and do I care?

Hair in the morning
Hair at night
Oh my gosh–my house is a sight

Hair on the lampshade
Hair on the couch
People want to know why I'm such a grouch

Oh, and there goes a feather!

Hair
By Marjorie Meanger

I, Marjorie Meanger, have been blessed with a healthy head of hair with a slight curl that makes it easy to maintain. I would like to say I am a woman who enjoys short hair. I have had my hair short for most of my life, with the exception of the years that my mother rolled my hair in long curls that hung down on my shoulders. I have always admired beautiful, long, bouncy hairstyles that look so glamorous. The problem is that as soon as I let my hair grow out, I can't stand it and run for a haircut. Great Clips is my favorite because I just walk in and am taken care of in short order. I get a haircut approximately every six weeks and wash and blow dry it daily.

The Lord has been very kind to me by allowing me to keep the same hair color all of the past seventy-three years, and now, I have just a touch of graying. My family genes also enter into that blessing, for which I am forever grateful.

Back in 1955, when I was a freshman at Northern Illinois University with swimming as my first class, I decided I needed a permanent home. My dear mother tried to discourage me, but I persuaded her to give me a very gentle Toni permanent. Needless to say, Mom knew best. The end product was a brunette Little Orphan Annie. It was so curly that I cried and did not want anyone to see me. I returned to campus and got a trim the same day, which helped some. So that was the first and last permanent in my life. The moral of the story: Mother knows best.
My hair has been low maintenance and low budget. I have friends who have spent countless hours and dollars for permanents, coloring, shampooing, and setting. I am grateful.

Postscript: Marge's hair is one of fairy tales. Dark, shiny, and lovely. She always looks well-coiffed. Her practical approach to hair is refreshing and grounding. It is no wonder this woman is someone my two grown children say they admire in our church.

Hair

By Linda Papanicholas

H *Here today*, gone tomorrow. Trying not to get too attached to the hair on my head.
Always changing. From pixies to page boys to the Dorothy Hamill and Farrah Fawcett dos. My hair has endured
many perms, cuts, and styles. I'm quite pleased it hasn't all fallen out.
I *Imagine…*Life without hair issues. If you don't have it, you want it. If you have too much, you want less. Curly wants
straight, Straight wants body. Surely, this is entertaining to God!
R *Reminiscent.* Remembering the beautiful, natural highlights of yesteryear when I saw my daughter's hair. Highlights
that can only come from a bottle now.

✝✝✝

Twizzler

By Pam Stare

"Perfect," I thought sarcastically when Paula announced our first essay was to be on hair. Of all the topics that could have been chosen or an essay in a Bible study, "hair" was not one that I would have guessed, although I immediately had some ideas about what I would write.

I do not have good hair, and like other women that I've spoken to, I spend far too much time (and money) on my hair. For as long as I can remember, my hair has occupied an inordinate amount of my time and effort.

One of my kindergarten friends had beautiful braids, so I decided that I'd grow out my ponytail and have braids too. One of the aspects of my "bad" hair is that it grows really slowly, so the growing process to get these braids that I coveted took a long time…and then there was the sad realization that, unlike my playmate's gorgeous, thick braids, I had braids that looked like brown Twizzlers! Apparently, I expected my hair to grow both long and thick, simultaneously. It may have been at that point that I cut my long, fine hair for the first time.

Throughout my life, there have been many similar disappointments with my hair as I tried to make bad hair good or at least stylish. I was VERY successful with my first introduction to hair products, however. For me, that first product was hair spray and lots of it. My ability to tease and spray my hair was unmatched, as evidenced by a group picture where my hair was so big that my otherwise round face looked like a pea, and the person standing behind me was nearly totally obscured. I did love that era, though, because once my hair was teased and sprayed, I didn't have to do much with it for days except to keep it shaped sort of round. If you're laughing right now, it's because you've lived through that fashion season as well… The next hairstyle that I remember required sleeping on brush rollers that left dents in my head. Seriously. That pain was equal to, but not greater than, the pain of pulling all of my hair into a ponytail on top of my head, wrapping it around orange juice cans, and scotch-taping down my bangs for the perfectly straight hair look that lasted only until the first breath of humidity touched it. Then, all bets were off. Most likely, I'd have some version of a Roseanna Danna hairstyle, which was only fun if the hair could be removed after the skit was done. Mine could not.

Along with all these struggles with hairstyles, I also had to struggle with the fact that I started to have grey in my hair in my early 20s. By the time I was 30, my hair was salt and pepper, and I didn't like it. Businessmen with salt and pepper hair were distinguished.

Businesswomen with salt and pepper hair were old. For many years after I first started coloring my hair, the first place that I sought when I moved to a new city was to find the hair salon that carried my products. I panicked more than once when my stylist left, fearing that my color would never be right again.

Looking back on all of this makes me laugh, but it also makes me realize again how petty and shallow I am. God did not give me the gift of great hair. Though I have been aware of that for most of my life, it's been a long, slow process for me to try to identify and develop the gifts that He gave me. If I spend as much time working on that as I have spent working on my hair, spiritual growth should be amazing.

✝✝✝

Hair
By Kristin Fischer
2009

I was a pixie for almost half my life. Yes, I was one of those girls with super short hair, carefully sculpted around the ears and shaped to a perfect point in the back, otherwise known as a pixie cut (think Twiggy, Mia Farrow, Peter Pan).

My mother had drilled into my sister and me (yes, she had one, too) the belief that we had such beautiful faces that we shouldn't cover them up with all that hair. We bought into this for far longer than we should have.

For years, I would grow my hair out for a while, only to tire of it and chop it all off. When I had my first child at 27, I let my hair grow longer, mainly because it was just too hard to find the tie to get it cut. Lo and behold, I looked pretty good with long hair! I wore a ponytail for the first time in my life when I was 28.

The years passed, and I spent many happy hours braiding and styling the hair of my three daughters. They are three and four years apart, so they went through various hair stages at different times. When Lauren was in middle school, I dried and curled her hair every day before school. I was lucky to get Sally and Tess to wash and or comb their hair at that point. By the time Lauren reached high school, she could do her own hair plus French-braid Sally's while I did Tess'. We spent a lot of time making sure there were no "bumps" when we did ponytails. Now, if I could only figure out how to do it for myself without ending up with "dents".

Recently, my sister and I were despairing over my mother's hair. She has always worn it in some form of pixie cut (what a surprise, right?) I have a theory. If you see a young girl with a really short haircut, you can be certain her mother will have one that almost matches. The reverse for long-haired young girls does not hold true.

Anyway, my mother is on television every week as a member of the city council, and her hair is always a disaster. My sister has tried showing her how to blow dry it, use a curling iron, hair products, and anything to get it under control, all to no avail.

As we talked, a light bulb went on. Hey, wait a minute! Katy and I didn't have beautiful faces that shouldn't be covered up! My mother was just absolutely clueless about hair, and that was her easy out! All those years of ponytails, hot rollers, and updos that I missed out on. All the boyfriends I could have had with my long, waist-length hair!

Well, I'm making up for it now. Yes, I will probably be that woman who has a ponytail way beyond it is age-appropriate.

✝✝✝

Heir
By Michele Claney

As I age, I spend more time inspecting my hair. Is it getting grayer? Is it fading? Truth be told, I have convinced myself that the more expensive shampoo I buy is actually better for my hair color. When I cheaped out and bought a more inexpensive shampoo, I thought that my hair was not as dark. Really, it's true.

I compare my hair to my mom's as I have been told that I looked like her, and compared to her my whole life, I feel that my hair will age as hers did. So far, that seems to be a pretty accurate theory. My mom died 17 years ago, right before her 54th birthday. She did not color her hair, and I don't know if she would have. However, her hair was definitely getting *some* gray in it. I really only started doing this aging comparison thing when other people brought it up. The closer I get to her final age, the more I take notice of how she aged. I see myself changing, and I see her in myself. It's not just my face and hair; it's my hands, too. I feel the arthritis creeping in and my joints getting bumpy like hers. Her age is frozen, and mine keeps getting older. I'm catching up to her. For now, my mother is my aging barometer. In a few years, I will be aging on my own. It is yet another part of her that will no longer be a part of my life.

It is odd sometimes to resemble someone so much. I have had people know who I must be even though they haven't met me. A couple of times, her friends have looked at me with tears in their eyes because they see her in me. Sometimes, it's hard to see yourself in someone else. Now, I occasionally catch a glimpse of myself in a mirror, and it strikes me. For some reason, it usually catches me off guard.

I consciously decided a long time ago that I would never have the hairstyle my mom had when she died because it would be too much. I want to reserve that final image of her in my head and not let it blur into my own.

Postscript: When this was read in class, everyone cried. No one spoke for a long time.

✝✝✝

Hair
By Paula Dettman

I will be so glad when this project is over! It has consumed large amounts of time thinking about all things hair. Somehow, the longer I thought about hair, the more scattered my thoughts became, causing both laughter and tears as I ended up reminiscing…

Looking at scripture about hair, I ended up reading 1 Corinthians 11, discussing women covering their heads in worship. Verse 6 says if the woman does not cover her head, she might as well cut her hair, and since it is a shameful thing for a woman to shave her head or cut her hair, she should cover her head… It amazes me how the Bible can be so comforting, while at other times, it can be so upsetting to me!

This causes me to remember how my ex-husband would not hear of me cutting my very long hair while we were together. After we split, I went to "get the ends trimmed," --as that had not been allowed. I didn't have a regular hairdresser as I would go to where it was the cheapest for a trim, so I decided to go to the shop that was close. God always seems to put the people you need in your path, and I met Heide, who had just got her license and started working. When I told her to "trim a little off the ends," her reply was, "What? Your hair looks terrible. You do know that you won't die if you cut your hair?"

Needless to say, that was _exactly_ what I needed to be told, and she cut a lot more than the ends off. Twenty-nine years later, she is still cutting and coloring my hair, and I am grateful she is in my life.

Hair can be powerful (others using it to control us as well as it letting us control others) when really in the scope of life; why should it? For me, it seems that hair has become like so many areas of my life as time passes. What was so important and fun when I was young is not so important or fun now. It used to be such fun to get my hair done, and when I left the shop, I felt great. Now, I wonder why I am spending so much money, and I am still not happy with how I look. (maybe because of my weight, my hearing aids, my headache…)

With all of the frustration this project has caused, there has also been the joy of thinking about how, the second time around, God put a kind, loving Christian man in my path. He encourages me to try whatever I want and doesn't get upset with the way things go. I thank God every day for the countless blessings he gives me: Lee and all the things in life that truly matter. BUT I am still waiting on the answer to 'What to do with my hair?"

Postscript: When read to the class, they were amazed at her poignant transparency. VERY quiet, close to the vest, Paula D rocked the evening class.

 ✝✝✝

Hair

By Carol Harris

When I woke up this morning and got out of bed, I looked out the window to see what the weather was like. Rain again-which would mean another bad hair day. As I thought about my day and what I needed to get done, I knew that I needed to spend time writing my hair essay for Bible Study. I also needed to spend time fixing my hair for the day. This essay made me realize how much time and money I spent on my hair. I know we all want to have great hair, and we spend a lot of time fixing it every day. But do we spend that much time praying? Do we spend that kind of money on giving to more important Christ-directed activities?

Yes, I do believe that God accepts us and loves us no matter what our hair looks like. Just as it is said in the Bible in 1 Peter, it reminds us that we should be known for the beauty that comes from within; the radiant beauty of all is spiritual beauty. I do think hair is somewhat important; very often, it is a way to express ourselves and makes us feel good. The word hair is mentioned many times in the Bible. Hair was talked about, but I am sure that God would not want us to spend so much time worrying about how our hair looks every day. God does not care what we look like on the outside—God looks at our hearts. We should be putting more or our extra time into prayer.

I believe that even through hair, it is a lesson from God teaching us to accept that with each day, God is by our side. God is reminding us that "hair" is just 'hair". Good hair day or bad hair day—God loves us just the way we are.

Postscript: Twelve years later, Carol is grandmother to twin girls, and a few weeks prior to their birth, her mother died from cancer. She had fought for a year and lost her hair. They were very close. Carol puts a lot of time in prayer. When I read her essay, it hit me that "hair" and "prayer" rhyme. Her faith journey has brought her to become a prayer warrior. She shared with me that she had not colored her hair in a while—she did not have time for all the activities of babies and visiting her dad. I believe her essay should be named 'Hair Prayer'.

Grace in the Mystery

†

Deborah by the Palm Bible Study: Ecclesiastes
2013

"Meaningless! Meaningless! says the Teacher, utterly meaningless....and there was nothing gained under the sun."
- Ecclesiastes 1:2, 2:11

What is good? This is the question I posed to my class as we traversed the words of the Teacher in Ecclesiastes. Ecclesiastes is the hard, even dark side of faith. It reduces you to your knees. As a teacher, I wondered, "Why teach a book of the Bible when it is so hard to find Christ within its pages?" Then, a thought occurred to me: "Why would you need Good News if you only acknowledged religious fulfillment and glorious joy within the boundaries of religion?"
Under the sun, the author of Ecclesiastes teaches that pleasure, wealth, career, status, and even wisdom are meaningless. The word translated as "meaningless" is "level" in Hebrew. "Hevel" to the ancient Hebrews meant "smoke, steam, vapor, breath," yet the metaphor is lost in the English translation. The Teacher is not saying that life is meaningless but that it is confusing. Like a thick fog or swirling smoke, our life can be disorienting when we cannot see or understand it.
The Teacher keeps his eyes on humanity's view of futility, but he also ultimately recognizes God's reign in the world. When writing the essays, some struggled with humanity; others struggled with

91

God.

What if God is not the problem? What if our expectations of God are the problem? We have expectations of what God will do in our lives. We don't know God for who he is. What if we have the wrong image of God? Ecclesiastes discusses who we are in God's big story; we may not always like how the author unravels the thread. This is why it's important to consider the question, "What is good?" Only then can we truly understand life under the sun.

What is Good?

By Sharon Kay Wadelin

Simply said... everything is good. Sometimes, you have to look deep and hard to find it, but I believe it because I have faith. I have confidence that God works in everything for our good.

"For I know the plans I have for you, they are plans for good and not for disaster, to give you a future and a hope." Jeremiah 29:11

Those plans include doing what we know is right, showing compassion to others, and walking with Him daily--for what is what He has told us is good.

It is good for humankind to understand that Christ experienced temptations and injustices just as we do, but that because of His victory over death, we can have eternal life if we choose to love and follow Him.

We should fear God and do his work while on earth. Once we admit that all is in God's hands, then our prayers and praise will help us accomplish the great mission of bringing others to Christ. As we pursue good, we allow others to see God in our lives.

*Being a good follower begins and ends with a dependence on the daily guidance of our Heavenly Father. *

- Postscript: Sharon W's life verse is Jeremiah 29:11.

The Grace of Music

DB ✝P Evening Class

Music is Magic
By Joshua Fredrickson

I was at a party a few years ago when my film buff friend walked up to me with the dreaded question: "Seen the new Hobbit movie? It is amazing!"

Ugh! "Not yet...Umm...how about those Bears?" (I have learned to change the subject quickly)

See, I don't get much traction when I tell people I don't like Harry Potter or The Lord of the Rings stories. A bunch of pimply kids running around with capes and magic wands yelling "Expelliarmus" (ex-spell-ee-arm-us). Ugh, give me a break. Of course, I am in the minority. People love these movies. Especially, my wife. Sorry, all that magic voodoo mumbo-jumbo is just not for me. Maybe I just saw too many creepy Doug Henning specials as a kid.

My son asks if magic is real, and I respond in a defiant tone, "No, I believe in hard work and elbow grease." I should probably humor him and his imagination more. I'm not totally curmudgeon; I do believe there are divine miracles, and I do believe in personal experiences that go beyond understanding. With that said, one thing that is amazing (almost to the point of thinking it is magic) is music.

Music does some amazing things. If I'm a little restless at night (bedtime), I often flip to a light classical music station; it can almost instantly calm my nerves and lull me to sleep. Bringing this back to the bible, I think of King Saul. After God had left him, Saul became restless and called for music to be played. It was David (the author of all those psalms) who came and played his lyre for him. And the Bible says:

"David would take up his lyre and play. Then relief would come to Saul: he would feel better, and the evil spirit would leave him". Samuel 16:23

See? Magic!

I do like music, and if I were to list all the songs that can "magically" change my mood in a heartbeat, we would be here all night. Here are just a few. To me, nothing can make you reflect on your family and your often misguided priorities more than the song "Cat's in the Cradle" by Harry Chapin. Hearing "The Wreck of the Edmund Fitzgerald" by Gordon Lightfoot reminds you of how fragile life is. If you want to be inspired by the innocence of youth, listen to Cat Steven's "Moonshadow." And if you forget your need for God's salvation, nothing can stir the soul to repentance as a good rendition of John Newton's "Amazing Grace," especially when it is played with bagpipes.

I do like music, and I like all different genres. And while I would not put country music on my iPod rotation, there is a certain twangy song that sticks with me. It is "I Hope You Dance" by Lee Ann Womack (Wow-mack)

If you don't know it, the song is a cute little tune about a parent's hope and desire for their children's future. For me, it is specifically touching as it was the song for the daddy-daughter dance at our wedding. See, before you get married, there is that moment in the engagement when it finally sets in– "Hey, I'm getting married. Wow. This is it. There is no turning back."

That didn't happen when I asked for my parents' permission when I got down on one knee. Not when we booked the church or even at the rehearsal dinner. It happened the day before the wedding, on the way back from picking up the tuxedo, and that twangy song came on the radio. Instantly, the reality set in. What a feeling. I thought, *The next time I hear that song will be after our wedding.* God would have created a new entity. I will no longer be Joshua; I will be one-half of the Fredrickson Couple–the start of a new family with a new beginning.

On our wedding day, while everyone in the sanctuary heard the bridal march song played by Mark Edwards on the organ– in my head, as Courtney angelically walked down the aisle with her father right next to her, I heard Womack's country song in my head. My father-in-law handed off a beautiful daughter who meant the world to him with his trust and a fatherly request that I would continue to make sure *she would dance.* A tidal wave of emotion in a small moment, an instant mood-changing experience that defies explanation–that is magic, and that is music. Paul reminds us:

"Husbands, love your wives, as Christ loved the church and gave himself up for her…" - Ephesians 5:25

With a lot of God's guidance and an occasional spin of Womack's country music song magic, I will do my best to make this happen…

Especially when I find myself at 2 am, after seeing the opening night midnight showing of "Harry Potter and the Goblet of waste-my-time" movie.
On the way home, my wife (beyond giddy) turns to me and says, "Honey, wasn't that the best movie ever?" I hold her hand and say, "Yep… It was a good time. Expelliarmus!"

Postscript: Joshua and Courtney are a magical couple. Courtney is exuberant and expressive. Joshua is an ever-practical engineer with leadership skills that have advanced the gospel in the church and community. (Courtney, too, has done more than her share to share the gospel.) Their children, Charlie and Nora, are one of our favorite dinner guests, along with their parents. They are polite, engaging conversationalists. Their family is dancing and showing others how to also.

Music for Me
Essay by David Hall
DB†P Evening Class

My first memory of music was in 1964, listening to Petula Clark while throwing rolled-up socks in an old lampshade. At five years old, I did not understand the importance of quickness or jumping ability as it related to the game of basketball, but I sure seemed to be quicker and jump higher when listening to the words of "Downtown."

Later in my youth watching the smile of my aunt while she listened to Motown always brought a smile to *my* face.

Obtaining a driver's license gave me an opportunity to sing out loud without being a nuisance to others. I loved the way music inside a very old Volkswagen beetle made me feel invisible, turning up the volume as if no one else could see me.

I enjoy all types of music, including country music. During my freshman year at Butler University, I was asked by some city slicker what kind of music I liked. I responded, "Both kinds: Country and Western."

Brother Hershel was a Southern Baptist preacher who spoke at my grandmother's funeral. Hershel and I shared a couple of things in common: 1. We loved the Lord, and 2. Neither of us could sing. During his thoughtful sermon, he said how much he was looking forward to going to heaven because he knew God was going to "tune him up" when he arrived. I also look forward to that day!

Stimulating Grace

Hebrews 10:24-25 "And let us consider how to stimulate one another to love and good deeds, not forsaking our own assembling together, as is the habit of some, but encouraging one another; and all the more as you see the day drawing near." NASB 1995

Some people make life better. Some people push you to make new discoveries, encouraging a more vibrant life of deep reflection. You can learn so much from examining your thoughts and voicing your questions. This is the blessing I received through an email conversation between me and another Paula.

I will respectfully call her #1 and myself #2. She is a vibrant magnet of a woman. Paula #1 is a whirling ball of energy, making sure she engages with each person she sees when she walks through the threshold of our Church. Her voice stands out from the crowd, and it's clear that the Spirit is alive within her.

From the moment I met her, I knew I would be in her entourage. I had to be known as the #2—not the First Paula. I wonder if she is Sylvia Wallin's ambassador 30 years later in this church? Sylvia was the one who steered and cleared the way for me when I moved to St. Charles, Illinois. Although fifty years my senior, she made sure I had a pathway made clear to navigate the entry into a new community and church.

The email exchange occurred after I emailed her a Monday devotion.

Thu, Aug 4, 2022 at 8:09 AM

Good morning #2!

I'm here reading and contemplating Philip Yancey's book "The Jesus I Never Knew," and it just occurred to me that I think I've missed something that you probably know... What was it that occurred to those young men, those ordinary Joe's (the disciples) to convince them to just up and leave their wives, mothers, friends, synagogues, livelihoods, homes, towns... to follow a HOMELESS STRANGER and travel what must have seemed willy-nilly from one town to another, preaching a message that was COMPLETELY foreign to what they'd ever heard, who hadn't even claimed to be God yet. I mean, the Holy Spirit had not yet arrived. Jesus had not performed any miracles yet. And since He was a man, a human, what was it? Charisma?

HELP!!!! #1

✝✝✝

Aug 4, 11:39 AM

Dear #1,

I have been puzzled about the disciples following Jesus, too. However--through the years as I have a similar question to various people (pastors/academics/friends), and this is what I have come away with:

1. It was not a one-time meeting with Jesus that brought the men to their decision. They had seen and heard His teachings more than one time. John the Baptist, too--had been on the scene.

2. Nowhere does it say that their family members protested...and it is not recorded in Scripture that they were "thrilled", but there is not a word about the protest. So...Jesus was special.

3. Compare this to Abraham. He was credited with being righteous for faith. Can FAITH be so convicting that it will allow someone to change a life to a radical degree? Abraham did. It did Moses--even before the burning bush--he saved the Hebrew slave and ran from his life of luxury. What about Rahab? FAITH. "For faith is the substance of things hoped for, the evidence of things not seen."

4. Charisma? If by this you mean Jesus was compelling: YES! Fully divine, fully human...that would set you apart.

5. I don't believe the disciples thought it was a vague mission--although they did not know "THE MISSION" – they had faith in God's plan.

I don't know the answer to "What made them drop their ordinary lives to do something extraordinary?" --but I believe it is rooted in faith.

Thanks for asking, dear friend...

#2

Aug 4, 8:31 PM

Thank You, Paula #2!! It would be interesting to know how their families survived while the disciples were away for so long. All we can know is that God provided. And I, for one, pray that I would have up and followed Him too.

Dear #2,

Aug 6, 12:06 AM

Thoughts for today...I have also STRUGGLED with the words of Jesus' Sermon on the Mount. Every time I read or thought of them, I felt a true sense of DREAD.

So much so that I wondered, 'What is the point? I can't ever achieve or continue with any of these, so why keep trying?' Well, because I LOVE Jesus and deeply desire to at least get to the fringes of Heaven! Then comes His promise of Grace. WHEW!!! But how many times can I be forgiven, especially for the SAME SINS??!!!! Why don't I GET it?

Well, those thoughts are a revolving door...and yes, I have and continue to learn about our Precious Lord, and while doing just that, today, as I read Philip Yancey's "The Jesus I Never Knew," I FINALLY GOT IT....

Have you ever read this book? In chapter 7, where he writes about Tolstoy & Dostoevsky and their opposite perspectives...WOW!!! His summary on pg. 144.... AMAZING!!! I feel MUCH better now and hungry for SO MUCH MORE!!!

Should be prescribed reading for ALL Christians.

~#1

(#1 always signs her email with a flag, a saguaro cactus, and a cute sun/desert/saguaro scene)

Aug 8, 11:23 AM

Dear #1,

I read the SOM this morning. (thankful you prompted me to do this) and I asked myself, "What brings me joy/gladness while reading, and what is troubling?" I took notes on each section—assurance and trepidation.

That is where Yancy puts this struggle into perspective. EVERYONE is on ground level with grace over us. Being used to "drag" us into safety, we have no fear. Does this make sense?

Peace, #2

August 8, 4:17 pm

Dear #2

I understand all except 'Being used to "drag" us into safety; we have no fear. '

August 10 7:02 AM

#1,

If we ever fear for our salvation--there should be none--as Yancy gives a visual--there is a "net of grace", and the net is always there--and it "drags" as a fishing net does--not losing a single fish. I think about a butterfly net my mom has--but she has caught a bat in it! It did not let the critter go--until she had it outside--it was "safely" returned to its outside habitat. That is how we are--safely returned by the net of grace that Jesus has provided to the Father, but like the bat, we have to be "dragged" to safety. (there was a bat that did NOT make it to safety–mom kind of took it to its doom since it had scared her in the middle of the night–the perils of country living–and she turned 80 this year!) This is a round-a-bat :) way of saying what I was thinking...

#2

Aug 10 9:23AM

#2,

Girl you got that RIGHT…DRAGGED is the word!!!

Grace through Trials

✝

One of our pastor's favorite authors is Walt Brueggemann, who says that no life is lived in a straight line. Instead, our lives go up and down, like a roller coaster or a bucking bronco ride. We alternate between three stages of faith: Orientation, Disorientation, and New Orientation. Brueggemann sees this pattern in the Psalms. King David traveled through times of Orientation, then times of Disorientation, and, finally, times of New Orientation.

One day, Pastor Larry was teaching on Brueggemann's insights in our class.

"In the Disorientation Psalms, we are given permission to BRING IT ON! And do we ever 'bring it on' to God!" Larry had captivated the group at this point. We were listening with rapt attention.

"I myself have gone through a time of deep depression or disorientation," Larry continued. "One day, I went to talk to a professional counselor.

The professional asked me, 'What is the source of your down-ness?' I told him, 'I just want to go back to my old self.'

He listened to me. Then the wise counselor said, 'Why do you want to go through the same *old crap?*'"

Pastor Larry continued, launching into a discussion of Exodus chapter 1. He spoke of the story of the oppression of Israel in Egypt. They became slaves, and then Moses set the exodus in motion. As their greatest prophet and their lawgiver, he rescued them from Egypt.

As we know, the Israelites were disobedient and unhappy with the exodus, even though it was their physical and spiritual redemption journey. They were grumblers and mumblers. They often wanted to give up and go back to their slavery in Egypt (Exodus 15:22).

"There is always a 'back to Egypt committee' in every church," Larry said.

Ouch. Double Ouch.

This story stunned me as I sat there. It felt very personal because of a situation I was facing. My emotions were brittle. Yet I continued engaging with Larry and his own vulnerability about his experience with the counselor. I watched the crowd in the room. I could see the others taking his words and being moved deeply. This sharing of pastoral knowledge was more than words.

"Israel, like us, was not asking, 'How should I transform myself as a redeemed person?'" said Larry. "They simply wanted to return to the same old crap, as my counselor would say. But in the process, their freedom would be forfeited. Rather than wanting to go backward, we should look for ways to become agents of change during times of disorientation.

"We are meant to be agents of change, even in the midst of disorientation. The insights that come to us are not for us only. We must be agents of change—light, salt, leaven—like Jesus taught. Are you being this agent of change, even in the midst of disorientation?"

This thought resonated with me.

I am to be an agent of change. Like salt! I had never thought of this before! How did I miss this for so long? I often thought only about how salt tasted, not about how it was utilized in the world. Now, I was thinking about this passage in a new way.

"Where is your life?" Larry asked.

He mentioned a few places we might be:

- Are you on an interstate? - Orientation
- A cul-de-sac? – Disorientation
- Detour? — Disorientation
- Trial? — Refining Orientation
- Under construction? -- Moving towards New Orientation
- Is it where the sun is clearly out?—Orientation
- Or in Toils and Snares, a place of Disorientation like our opening hymn, Amazing Grace, described.

A stillness enveloped the room as Larry described these places of pain and disorientation. The hush was only interrupted by a creaking of chairs. We listeners all wanted to know our location and how to progress towards God.

Pastor Larry reminded us that we do not have to change our address to experience disorientation. It can happen to any of us at any time. Everyone tries to keep away disorientation by putting safeguards in place: money in the bank account, a healthy family, settled feelings, peace on our street, peace on earth, peace in the family." But this is not always possible.

However, it *is* possible to wait on God during times of pain. Rather than complaining about our difficulty, we can wait for God's New Orientation to arrive.

"Don't you believe that God is at work?" Larry challenged us. "Let God show you something NEW.' That's what I mean by New Orientation. In New Orientation, the sun comes out. There is renewal, discovery, birth, joy, and appreciation (see Psalm 23).

"In the Easter story, there is darkness before dawn. When Judas is with Jesus at the last supper, and Satan enters him, he leaves, and 'it was night.' (John 13:30) Darkness will enter life at some point, but the dawn awaits the faithful."

BIG POSTSCRIPT:

A few days after Larry shared this teaching, he and I spoke in the hall before church. He expressed that he had not been feeling well the day he taught the class. He thought it was his medication. I assured him I didn't notice any difference in the presentation, but I did notice that he looked tired by the end of the second class. Pastor Larry had a stroke one week after being our guest speaker. He died a week after the stroke.

Disorientation. Tears. Prayers. Where can I go to meet God? This is an application of disorientation I was not expecting.

Change is something you can count on.

The Grace of Perspective

✝

Perspective is often confused with the word *prospective*.

Perspective is a way of regarding circumstances or topics or points of view.

Prospective is an adjective meaning "likely to happen at a future date."

My *perspective* on *prospective* events in my life is clouded by my past.

When looking back on my past, I could write like author Anne Lamott, who writes about what most of us don't like to think about—she does not sugarcoat sadness and loss, and she tosses in dark humor. I could make gritty subjects of life all bare and gripping. Readers would grab the book and draw it in a little closer, making sure each detail is taken in. Raw, edgy memory fragments could become emotional for the writer and the reader. Scandalous betrayals are juicy on pages, but collateral damages occur. Perhaps if sadness, anger, sabotage, and fear started radiating from the story, this would bring the reader closer and closer to the page.

Memory fragments have sharp edges, like pieces of broken glass. But I must wrestle, as Jacob did, to perceive the ragged, sharp edges *not* as harmful and cutting but as puzzle pieces that fit together and assist in sanctification. They have a purpose in eternity.

Instead of focusing on the pain, I focus on the beauty. I would like to have the spirit of another "author, Ann," assist me: Ann Voskamp. She writes in gratitude. She is the Bezalel and Oholiab of word-beauty. Rather than focusing on the negative, I want the loveliness of my language the imprint of my story, to bring lasting joy and beauty to others. There are countless ways God's grace and love profoundly work—from my perspective.

There are pretty stories and not-so-pretty stories. Both have value. Both bring truth to light. My story will be more Voskampy. Less Lamott.

Back to being Anne Lamott. Cruddy things happen. Sickness occurs. People die. Relationships dissolve. Money is loved more than people and God. Wretchedness is not just for the movies.

One day, I had a painful conversation with a cosmopolitan friend. As she and I were chatting, she commented on my upbringing: "I picture farm life as enduring isolation and going to the city to get supplies once a year."

This farm girl felt embarrassed and couldn't articulate a reply. Finally, I mumbled something like, "Yeah, we went to the city to stock up... it was a big day," with a slight laugh.

Is this friend thinking I had better hitch up the wagon and get home before dark? I was humbled and provoked... I knew now what her perspective was of my life. The geographical location of my early life and television movies had clouded her assumptions of me. It was no use trying to change her mind on what was ingrained. In her city experience, she had seen country folk identified as simple people who could not fully escape nor have the luxuries of her megalopolis living. Why did I suddenly feel ashamed and a little put out by her absurdity? My own insecurities.

But I began wondering how I could see this awkward conversation as an instrument of grace.

Is God provoked when I say ridiculous things to him like my friend said to me? Does God think I had better hitch up my sin and get praying?

God loves order. Yet, living life as a Christ-following, God-trusting Kingdom dweller is messy. There is not a day in my life when my mind, body, and soul have been completely "in order." When have I been perfectly righteous, completely in sync with God to the point of faultless communion? God is patient with me. And I can learn to be patient with my friend.

God says of me, "For I will forgive their wickedness and will remember their sins no more." Hebrews 8:12

God remembers my sin no more.

I am very imperfect, and I see the world through a foggy, sometimes inaccurate lens. My mind wanders. I get balled up over nothing–and something. I assume absurd things about others. People assume obtuse things about me. Cruddy things happen again and again. Sometimes, my perspective is limited to staring in a mirror, seeing only myself and my desires. My insecure perspective needs to be righted that I may be the grace distributor, not the self-pitying whiner. Like LaMott in her book Bird by Bird, I will get on with it. Her brother had writer's block when writing an essay on birds. After the boy had several attempts, their father gave the simple advice to go "bird by bird." Same for me. May my outlook peer forward steadily.

The good, the bad, and the ugly are woven through life's road, lived out in relationships—all of them. Yet, as we see the broken edges of relationships, we must remember The Grace. The bad and ugly remain, but they do not have the power necessary to damage.

We must change our perspective. Then, we are able to see the broken edges as an unfinished puzzle in the image God is creating. The beauty is in the journey, one step at a time. Thank you, Ann and Anne.

The Grace of a Wise Guide

Tempe, AZ
2020

Blessed are the meek, for they shall inherit the earth.
Matthew 5:5

"If you were to navigate through a minefield, wouldn't you want a map?" – Reverend Philip Dripps.

When we enter dangerous or difficult parts of our lives, we need a guide. We need a guide that has experience traversing the field of life that has minefields. That is what my pastors have been for me: guides.

In each season of life, God has given me mentors and guides during times of transition. They are unexpected escorts to direct and prod me. Pastor Kelly was the wise guide who helped me through a moment of conflict with a friend, helping me find true meekness.

Reverend Dr. Kelly B. Bender is a retired United Methodist minister. Preaching is his gift and his passion. He loves to share the radically unconditional grace of God revealed in Jesus Christ. His words have blessed me, encouraged me, and even disgruntled me, as every good rabbi does every once in a while.

One day, Pastor Kelly Bender stood up to preach a sermon on the Beatitudes.

"Each of the beatitudes begins with 'blessed are...'" Kelly said. "What does it mean to name ourselves as blessed? To name ourselves as blessed is to recognize there is a Giver behind the gift. And it is not us."

Beatitudes. Good enough. This will be a rerun. I will not have to listen intently...and I will be able to relax...

He said, "'Blessed are the meek.' The meek don't have to have their own way. The meek are more likely to listen first. They are more likely to understand and only later be understood. The meek are more likely to be collaborative. They are more likely to make decisions with people, not for people."

Wouldn't that be great? I thought from the pew. *If Pastor Kelly could only preach this to a few people I know.*

Yet, I was starting to squirm. Relaxing had not started.

"Being meek means I will be open to hearing something *outside* what I am convinced I already know. Being meek is counter-cultural. It's very easy to get tribal, to get defensive."

I thought about a friend with whom I had been having a not-to-be-named conflict. I knew I was the one who needed to learn meekness. *Oh Lord, he is getting to me now... does he know about 'you know who?'*

"You don't have to be wrong for me to be right," Pastor Kelly continued. He had hit a nerve.

Ok, I am getting it. Understanding comes slowly.

"We can learn and share our insights with one another because we have been freed to have an attitude of meekness. Not having to be right. Not having to have our way. This makes us more receptive to relationships, which makes it more likely to draw people near us. We need more meek souls..."

Oh, dear Lord, I take back all my non-meek thoughts. Help me be more like Pastor Kelly. To be meek, to be counter-cultural. I am being sorely tested. I am being tested in this very pew. I WANT to indulge in the opposite of meekness: sulking. I write this honestly because when I say and do the right thing, there is an inner self that is still there—that holds onto a deep sense of self-righteousness that is self-wickedness. Someone has hurt me. They need to be changed! I feel misunderstood and mistreated. I knew my thoughts did not spring from loving kindness and holy charity. I wanted to vindicate myself from the offender. That was a revelation of how little I knew of meekness. Would I learn here and now of His meekness? Jesus was despised, pierced, and crushed, yet did not open his mouth. What is this little incident of mine? Peter denied him three times, and a look of love–of meekness –brought him to repentance. And yes, Pastor Kelly, "Blessed are the meek, for they shall inherit the earth." Any righteousness given to me is a great favor on His part, so much for a rerun.

The Grace to Follow

✝

By Reverend Thomas Walker

From his memoir,

Tom wrote an extensive memoir, and he gave me a copy before he died. He told me how he wrote each morning and wanted to have his story for his family. It is deep, personal, and a real view of living as a man of God.

About twelve years into my ministry, a woman spoke to me one Sunday after church. She told me she really liked my preaching and that I always had something worthwhile to say. She said she often thought about my messages. "But," she added, "I think your preaching could be even stronger if you would take us inside some of the Bible stories and help us see our lives through those stories rather than just using them as a jumping-off point for the topics you want to bring to us."

It is hard for me to accept constructive suggestions from people because however well-intentioned they are, the ego in me hears them as criticism, as a need to improve or change when I think I am doing the best I can. When I went home and thought (some) more about what this woman was saying, I felt that she had an insight into something even more important than improving my preaching.

"Take us inside the Bible stories, and help us see our lives through those stories." It was an invitation, not just to shift the focus of my preaching, but a clue into how I might begin to know Jesus. This woman had opened a door and invited me to come through it.

The invitation I was hearing was to read the gospels. Read what those who knew Jesus said about him. Experience Jesus' words as they were recorded in the gospels. Step inside the stories, and with the power of imagination, be there in drama.

So, I began to read Mark's gospel. I chose Mark because it is generally agreed that this was the earliest gospel and reads straightforwardly, free from some of the embellishments of the other gospels.

As I read Mark, I stopped at the place in Mark (1:16-20) where Jesus called his first disciples, Simon and his brother Andrew, and then a few moments later, James and John. Simon and Andrew were fishing when Jesus came up to them. James and John were in a boat with their father, mending their nets.

As I lingered with this story, I felt myself being pulled into it. I could see the men on the beach, their tanned faces and calloused hands, working the nets, casting them out upon the open water, looking for fish. I pictured the men in the boat with their father carefully working to re-thread the weak and torn places in the nets that had been used so many times before. I felt the warm sunshine on my face and a light breeze blowing in from the sea. The men were all at work plying their trade, doing what they knew best. They laughed as they worked, injecting a bit of lightheartedness into the long hours and the struggles of trying to make ends meet, never knowing what price they would get for their catch and how much of it would be swallowed up by the heavy burden of Roman taxation.

They didn't see Jesus coming up the beach. Their backs were turned, their eyes focused on the work in front of them. *I* saw him because as I found myself in the story, I was off a ways from the boats up on a slight hill hidden behind some rocks and a tree. That's where I placed myself, close enough to see and hear everything, but far enough away so as not to be noticed. This was deliberate on my part, and it reflected my ambivalence about getting too close to Jesus. I wanted to see and hear him, but I was afraid of being approached by him.

First, he stopped to see Simon and Andrew. They turned around when they saw him. He engaged them in conversation, asking them about their fishing and how it was going for them. His words drifted over to me on the sea wind, and I heard him clearly as he invited Simon and Andrew to come with him. "Follow me," he said, "and I will make you fish for people." Mark 1:17

In the story, we are told that they immediately left their nets and went with him. Just like that. There was no hedging, no "Let me think about this," or "Let me go home and tidy up my household affairs," or "I'll get back to you in a couple of weeks." The story tells us they just left everything and went with him. I can't explain this. My twenty-first-century mind wants me to believe it didn't happen this way, that there must have been some delay between the invitation and the response. No one jumps immediately into a new situation without some hint of what they are getting into. And Jesus makes no promises, no guarantees, other than this one thing: *You will fish for people.*

I can try to rationalize the story and tell myself there are details left out, but you see, imagining myself in the story, being there, even hiding behind a tree, I must allow the drama to unfold as I read it.....

Who is this whose personal presence is so compelling that the men who were previously engaged in their work suddenly let go of it all to follow him? I found myself wanting to meet him, yet I would not venture out from my own hiding place. I watched, fascinated, drawn into the scene, yet afraid to get too close.

Then something happened. As I remained there with my own insecurities and fear, I saw Jesus walking away from the others and coming over to me. He had spotted me on the rise behind the rocks and the tree. He walked slowly over to where I was until he was standing directly in front of me. He looked at me intently. His eyes were gentle but piercing. I felt him seeing into my heart, and I knew he understood my struggle--the pulling away from him, yet the power in his voice and person drew me towards him. He called my name: "Tom." Then he said, *"You come too."*

Grace for Goodbye

✝

Reverend Tom Walker stood up to speak, his voice as gentle and calming as always. Though thirty years my senior, Tom had been a mentor to me over the years. His influence had poured over me like a waterfall. Always there to give advice, he'd been a guest speaker at our Bible Study many times. He was a mentor who provided wisdom with compassion. If I wrote him, he wrote back. If I called him, he picked up. If I walked up to him, his eyes smiled, and I knew he would engage me in conversation. I would like to believe this personal attention was for me only, but it was not. He was the shepherd of many sheep. Today, there was a packed house to hear him speak, as always.

But today, I knew he was giving his farewell discourse.

Tom began with a prayer. He told the congregation that he and his wife, Ellyn, would move to an extraordinary senior living village. They were moving by choice, not by event. The duplex would be larger than their current home, and he was excited. But his duplex would be an hour away.

My throat tightened and spasmed; the acid ran down from my mouth. *I don't want to be emotional. I know their new home is just west on the interstate.* Yet tears started to form as he spoke about the fifteen years of retirement and the challenges, how this church had been a blessing and a home to him. A new home would be an exciting adventure, but leaving would be a bittersweet experience.

Adios, my friends. Au Revoir. Sayonara. Arrivederci.

Goodbye is hard in any language.

My mind was reeling. *How does someone not in my peer group, not in my family, not my personal minister, not in my "friend" group, not my neighbor punctuate my life with an exclamation point?*

Tom's voice, naturally raspy, sounded gritty and apostle-like as he continued to speak. Tom had always had a great wealth of knowledge and experience, and he also possessed wisdom: the ability to discern inner qualities layered within relationships. The awareness of something more significant than the information presented. His remarks always overflowed with humility. I basked in it today, but I also shouted internally, *you can't leave me sitting in this pew!*

Reverend Tom Walker is like Moses--the humblest man. I will use superlatives because he is a superlative kind of man. He's approachable. He is the smartest pastor of pastors. He knows how to be a "minister." I respect him. When he speaks, he captures the crowd. He is not perfect by his admission. But the fact that he can define his weaknesses draws you into a relationship with him and enables you to examine your own faults closely. How can he be leaving?!

Coming back to the present, I heard that Tom was telling a story. "One of my best memories of growing up was the long summer days I spent playing baseball with the boys from the neighborhood in the vacant lot next to our house. We fashioned a ballfield with rocks to mark the bases. We kept the weeds down with

an old hand mower. The outfield fence was a garage across the alley at the back of the lot. That garage seemed to us as far away as the outfield walls in any.

Major league ballpark and it was rare for us to hit a ball over the garage. When it did happen, it was automatically declared a home run. Only two or three of us accomplished it, but I was one of them; when I saw a ball sailing off my bat over the top of that garage, I felt strong. As I look back now on those days long ago, I see how I lived then in a tightly-knit world. I felt secure in *my home* and at school, in our church, and on the ballfield next door. There was no sense of urgency about anything. No deep philosophical questions…. Just safety."

Tom related a passage to John 14:1-7, which says that Jesus is going away so he can prepare a place for us. He is creating a home for us. In order to arrive at that home, we must simply follow Him: the Way, the Truth, and the Life.

Tom explained that Thomas, the Doubter, didn't understand how to access this peace, this rest, this eternal home. Jesus explained that he is the Way, the Truth, and the Life.

 Now, my mind was whirling. If Tom wants me to catch all he is saying, this person-in-the-pew outfielder is having a hard time seeing the ball. That's good news. *I believe in Jesus, the Way, but I still feel most at home when Tom is with me!*

The baseball headed out of the park. Tom's words had smacked my thoughts, and they were getting mixed up with my emotions. I was screaming at God in my head right there in my pew, *Who will lead me now to YOU if Tom leaves!?* My throat was pulsing, and I wondered if I could hold all this in. I can't catch this hurling ball—too fast, too much spin.

Tom explains that a home is a safe place. Jesus has gone to prepare this safe place for us. In an ultimate sense, we are homeless here on Earth. We all have a longing for a different type of home. Not a physical place but a *spiritual place*. Everything on earth is fleeting, but we possess a sacred thirst, a quiet sorrow, and a deep longing that points us to our eternal home. This is a universal longing that happens to all people. That longing points to the home God has prepared. *Good Tom, really good,* I thought. *But I want you to stay. I am ready to catch the ball on the warning track at the top of the wall and call you out. You must stay and keep doing what you are doing.*

Tom ended his message by telling about a friend who helped him get to his home in the days before GPS. The friend met him at the interstate and showed him the way to his *home* through winding country roads at night. Tom followed.

A simple command: "Follow Me." That is what Jesus asks us to do. He is the way; if we follow him, he will take us *home.* The ball sails over the fence. A *home* run. My throat gives out. My eyes are wet. *Rockford is just an hour down the road.* Jesus' voice says, "Follow Me."

One day, we will join God in his Forever Home. Our hearts will truly rest in the rhythms of total acceptance.

 Jesus says in John 14:1-3, *"Do not let your hearts be troubled. You believe in God; believe in Me as well. In My Father's house are many rooms… I am going there to prepare a place for you. And if I go and prepare a place for you, I will come back and welcome you into My presence, so that you also may be where I am."*

God is working all the time to prepare us for that moment. This Sunday was no exception. Dr. Thomas J. Walker died on April 9, 2021, in Rockford, Illinois, at the age of 83.

Grace on Mount Nebo

✝

Bible Study Fellowship, Wheaton, Illinois
May 2009

We got to the end of Deuteronomy:

Moses—the prophet, teacher, leader, deliverer, the one who predicted the coming of Jesus Christ—DIED!! I cried my eyes out.

After forty weeks of studying the life of Moses in my Bible Study Fellowship women's group, it was heartbreaking to read of this great leader's death. It was like watching *The Titanic;* even though I knew the ending, it was a heart-wrenching experience, the death of this great man.

God and Moses were best friends: "Since then, no prophet has risen in Israel like Moses, whom the LORD knew face to face…" Yet He died. My tears flowed freely.

During the nine-month study, I had vicariously lived the life of Moses: prepared for his birth and adoption, watched the murder in my mind, fled with him into the wilderness, walked alongside him during his Midian years, cheered for him as he encountered God in the Burning Bush, suffered with him in the Exodus and forty years of wilderness wandering. But after all this camaraderie with Moses, I had to watch the devastating ending: Moses would never enter the promised land. Instead, he would die on the outskirts of the land.

Watching Moses' meekness as he received the bad news was heartbreaking. Moses had spoken his mind to the Creator of the Universe all his life. He had dialogued with God to the point of ridiculousness: "I can't speak well—find somebody else." He had interceded to the point of audacity: "Don't burn hot wrath against your chosen people…" Yet, when God gave Moses a view of the promised land and told him he would die and be gathered to his people, Moses did not argue with God's decision. Moses, the humblest man on earth, was content to go up the mountain to die with God.

The most committed of God's servants still must die. It is the common lot of men. Only two have passed out of this world into glory without fording the stream of death. And Moses is not one of the two. Since God is never unjust, I cannot forbid the Lord from calling home his own when it is time. Moses seemed to understand this, and he willingly accepted God's decision and kept his eyes on eternity. May Moses be our teacher in the art of dying. As we ponder his decease, may our fears be removed and our desire for heaven inflamed. May we all climb the mountain as willingly as Moses did.

Moses could accept death with grace because he knew death was not the end. Moses would live again. We all know there is a happy ending. Moses' fate is known. We have read about the Transfiguration, where Moses appeared on the mountain with Jesus and Elijah hundreds of years later. The three communed in brilliant holiness with Peter, James, and John, who witnessed the moment.

But right there, on Mount Nebo, Moses had to die.

I think about this passage at funerals. As I sit at the funeral of a loved one, I intellectually approve that a Resurrection is coming. I mentally understand that Moses would appear again at the Transfiguration, and I know that my loved one will appear again in the Resurrection. I profess faith in those moments.

However, this knowledge doesn't mean that Mount Nebo isn't painful. The visceral ache twists through my mortal body while my soul clings to the Spirit. I whisper, "It hurts, AND I KNOW THE ENDING. We will see Him face to face." For now, there is a symbolic mountain that we all must climb. We must enter the valley between Mount Nebo and the Mount of Transfiguration between death and Face-to-Face.

Moses died on Nebo, ready for the face-to-face. *"And Moses climbed Nebo from the plains of Moab to the top of Pisgah, across from Jericho... And Moses the servant of the LORD died there in Moab, as the LORD had said. He buried him in Moab, in the valley opposite Beth Peor, but to this day, no one knows where his grave is. Moses was a hundred and twenty years old when he died..." Deuteronomy 34:5-7a*

The Mount Nebo ascent allowed Grace to descend. Was there a sacred vessel God used to spill the unmerited favor over his servant as he scaled the summit? Showing obedience, Moses went up the mountain with no reserve, knowing his end was near. He viewed what he was not to possess and, for the last earthly time, had a dialogue with God, exhibiting grace to all future generations. Perhaps he used his own hand to bury and hold Moses.

For us, God uses time to bridge the chasm between Nebo and Face-to-Face. Time brings healing after a loss. Even though we often think: *Curse time. I need my comfort now in the present moment. I want that face-to-face moment to come now.* Time is a gift. It's the instrument that helps us draw close to Jesus. It's the tool that prepares us for the day we will see him face to face.

"The clock of life is wound, but once
And no man has the power
To tell when the hands
Will stop
At late or early hour
Now is the only time you own
Live, love, toil with a will
Place no faith in to-morrow
For The clock may then be still"
--handwritten note put in the family Bible
by my Grandmother (Ruth Elizabeth Morris)

The Grace of Practice

✝

1982, 2022

"May thy ball lie in green pastures
and not in still waters." -Ben Hogan

Golf in 1982

I can't believe I did it!

It was May 1982 and I headed to the golf course with deep relief. I had completed another year of rigorous university classes. I had persevered and made it through two years of pharmacy school. I had passed Pharmacy Calcs–the logarithm chart class–under Dr. Shaw's firm direction and Kristie's tutelage. A few years later, when I took the Pharmacy Boards, Calculations was my highest score; it was truly a miracle. God Bless Dr. Shaw.

The car ride to the course was the first time I felt relief in months. Not only relief but a sense of peace and well-being. Jim Croce played on the radio, David drove, and his friend Jeff rode in the front while my thoughts drifted in the back seat of the Toyota Corolla hatchback. I got out of the car–in my pink corduroy pants. Lordy, it was the 80s, and I picked up my pastel blue golf bag out of the car and followed the guys to the clubhouse. The play was unremarkable that afternoon, but not the unfettered feeling of ease. The sun quietly moved down in the west, and the grass was springtime limey-green. A quick nine holes before dark put us in a good mood, and we packed up. We ate pizza at Monical's. The Jim Croce lyrics linger in my mind:

"If I could save time in a bottle, the first thing that I'd like to do…"

The first thing I might do is put on a different pair of pants. Pink corduroy?

Golf in 2022

Summertime in Phoenix, and it was 6:23 a.m. David and I were teeing off on #2 on the links. We liked to go golfing early in the morning, then again in the evening to get nine more in. That morning, I was not wearing pink corduroy pants but a pink and black houndstooth skort and a sleeveless collared shirt with a club logo. A little nerdy still, but old nerdy. We played at a clipping pace, with David consistently scoring well and me… Well, let's say that my goal in this season of life was just to achieve some sort of hand-eye coordination.

I realized I had taken a forty-year hiatus from golf as we played. I'd been busy working, raising the kids, and following Jesus.

Forty years: a Biblical number, I pondered. The Israelites wandered in the desert for forty years, and the devil tempted Jesus for forty days. As for me, I spent those forty years waiting on God and honing discipline in my spiritual life, but not the golf life. I have resurrected the game after forty years with little change in score.

I had heard a golf quote by Ben Hogan that said, "Hitting a golf ball is the easiest thing in the world..." I wanted to cry when I heard this. To Mr. Hogan, a small white ball sitting on the ground– not moving– was very easy to strike. But it was easy for him because he had done it tens of thousands of times.

Something you do over and over becomes a habit, a routine. It becomes natural and "easy." Hitting a golf ball will probably remain a challenge to me at this stage of my life. However, some things are "the easiest thing in the world" because I have done them thousands of times. I have practiced them for the last forty years.

It is easy to speak of Jesus in daily life. It is easy to join a Christian fellowship, go to Bible Study, and worship on Sunday. It is easy to pray. It is easier to navigate the "hard things." I can teach many about Jesus. Christ's yoke is easy (Matthew 11:30).

Not all aspects of the Christian life are easy. Christians carry light burdens on a challenging road (Matthew 7:14). Love one's enemies.

Forgive seventy times seven? Regularly assume the role of a servant? Picking up a cross and denying oneself—is countercultural. Humans have an insatiable appetite for pleasure, comfort, and possessions. Delayed gratification makes me complain sometimes. The practice of denying self is directly from Jesus as an instruction to his disciples. It is not practiced by many modern Christians or understood by those looking in. I have the desires of my heart but have had to deny my own way of achieving them and do it God's way. While not easy, it grows easier through discipline and practice.

Forty years ago, I took Arnold Palmer's advice–not on golf, but on discipleship: "Practice is the only advice that is good for everybody." I'll flip a familiar golf adage: "In life, as in golf, it is the follow-through that makes the difference." We must begin to discipline ourselves and follow through until it becomes natural.

Later in the afternoon, Austin and Brandon joined us for nine. I missedthree short par putts. On the par fives, I had complete disasters. Iron play was for naught. On number nine, I chipped in the sand, only to flail it into another sand trap. Austin was even at this point; David and Brandon had ridiculously low number scores as I continued whirling around the green with my sand wedge and putter in the other hand. "Easiest thing in the world..." was not what I was thinking at that moment.

Yet, despite how hard golf was for me, my heart was light. I played golf with my son, son-in-law, and husband below Piestewa Peak on a sunny afternoon. My mind returned to the afternoon after I finished my second year of college. Forty years later, the unspoiled quietness of heart had gone deeper. The grace could be counted.

The grace poured over yesterday is as highly regarded as today. Like a symphony, each note is to be enjoyed.

Everything I do is assisted by grace. Working from the inside out, God brings every element of my being into harmony with the will of God.

If only that harmony would reveal itself in my golf swing.

Simple Graces

Phoenix, Arizona

Ecclesiastes 3:11
"He has made everything beautiful in its time. He has set eternity in the human heart, yet no one can fathom what God has done from beginning to end."

Signs of Grace are all around us.

We bought a house in Phoenix and decided to remodel it. We stripped the 50-year-old home down to the studs in some parts. After the drywall was torn out, we found the blueprints in the hallway. The original homeowner, a widower Jewish woman, Ruth, had moved from Cleveland and designed the home in 1978. Ruth had the same name as my paternal grandmother. With a little research, I found out Ruth and her second husband became influential in the community. They were active in the local synagogue and generous with their time and treasures.

Looking at the original blueprints, I began to appreciate the details the architect had included in the design. The over-the-window trim had seemed less-than-appealing when we bought it, but after I read the explanation on the prints, it became a favorite. I liked Ruth's choice of slump block, too. It was energy-efficient with a beautiful texture.

We had no idea about the energy-efficient part when we bought it. It's kind of like God's grace; we just fell into it.

It was reassuring to find these architectural prints. They were like a letter sent from the past—not written *to you*, but a message sent *for you*. This house was a beloved home. Once Ruth's, it was now the Hall House.

I knew I had to respond in some way to this lavish grace. So early one morning, before the carpenters arrived, I came to the house with Sharpie markers. I walked around the dusty, opened-up walls and considered this as more than a dwelling place. I prayed for blessings in our new home. Simple words, simple prayers. I wrote blessings on the studs that would be soon covered. Psalms, Proverbs, lines from the gospels, prayers. My favorite Bible verses in different marker colors are noted on the wood inside the drywall. I did not record what and where I put each verse or blessing. It is known only to the heavenlies *and* the next generation that will tear out the walls and find the faded phrases and blessings.

Later in the week, Rex, the carpenter, casually mentioned the writing inside the walls. I told him what I did and explained why. He liked the idea, and although he didn't profess to be a Christian, he did not reject the idea. A year later, Rex was working on a bathroom project at another property. I stopped by to drop off paint, and he said he wanted to share a picture with me: an angel in the clouds. The cloud-angel was beautiful.

"I wanted to see your face when you saw the picture," Rex said. The picture, if I can describe any part of it, was of clouds illuminated from behind, with a human-like apparition drinking coffee and looking over the shoulder toward earth. Rex stated he likes to capture cloud pictures, especially of supernatural occurrences. I believe the blessing I prayed over those studs may have opened Rex's eyes to the beauty of God's grace.

The blessing I prayed for the first days in my home has poured over me as well. Standing at the entrance of our home and glancing left (west), there are palm trees! FINALLY, A PALM TREE! DEBORAH IS REJOICING IN HEAVEN. Over the wall that forms the physical boundary on the west, I can see a tall steeple with a cross. Just like the Tyson Temple cast-aluminum spire overlooked my grace beginnings, I now had a tall steeple surveying my home, viewing my worship on Sunday, and endorsing perpetual grace.

Grace: God's favor. I picture grace as hues of purple pouring out of a white vessel that turns into wisteria, lavender, magnolia, lilacs, allium, and azaleas, dissolving into white-pink peonies as it tumbles over my circumstances. The fragrance is unbelievable.

Grace does not equal a perfect life. Grace does not mean gifts. It is clear in the New Testament. It is clear in the Old Testament. It is clear in my life. Grace is the simple things that God bestows on us, that he pours over every moment of our lives. He hides in the studs of our being, hoping we take the time to uncover it.

There is nothing difficult about grace. Nothing. It is compelling, not forced, this beautiful, favored gift. By ordained means–prayer, reading Scripture, communion– you will find His favor, but I hope this writing helps you find *The Grace* you were born into and walk in every day.

Every single day, every breath you take is a grace story. I will never be too old or too mature to experience a new work of grace. Christians never outgrow the need for a fresh outpouring of visceral awareness of grace. In all the chaos of this world, in all the hurt, there is a sense of heartfelt gratefulness. May the good news of God's free grace spread with contagion. May its effects be felt for many generations to come.

Grace of Naming

1962

My father's name was Paul, and my name is Paula. Mother said Paula was the only name Dad would consider for their firstborn if it was a girl. My name was ho-hum to me as a child. Bland. Nothing special. My mom's friend had a daughter named Tara Lynn. Hearing this southern Gone-with-the-Wind name made me think my name was so very ordinary. My imagination said, "If I had Tara Lynn as my name, I would be a lavish Hollywood star or a scientist making the next incredible discovery changing mankind. Paula, aka Tara Lynn, would rock the world!" I tried to tell my mom this, but it went unnoticed. Paula was perfectly suited to me, she said.

So, I will accept with gratitude my father's legacy. He taught me to embrace adventure, giving me a sense of strong fortitude and passed on the ability to turn ordinary circumstances into extraordinary—or maybe just odd and unusual. Maybe Tara Lynn would not have adapted to the non-Gone-with-the-Wind lifestyle I had.

Dad liked to travel, but to him, the journey was more important than the destination. To him, the main attractions were driving and talking to people at the gas stations and restaurants—not museums or national parks.

Dad's quirkiness came out in other ways. He didn't go to the dentist to get stitches from his extraction removed; he summoned the next-door neighbor (a policeman) to do it while his daughter held the field flashlight. Policeman John removed the stitches while Dad reclined in the lazy boy.

Dad took measurement to the next "level." He was more obsessed with levels than any carpenter. He would often carry a small level in his pocket or truck and give the tiny ones to my kids when they were little. They would come to the dinner table with their levels.

In addition, Dad was a scavenger. One thing he liked to acquire was Indiana limestone. Big slabs, little slabs. He would use his backhoe to dig up these giant rocks in neighboring places where people did not want the hindrance. This led him to his biggest leveling project. Shortly before he died, he took his large collection of limestone slabs and made an imitation Stonehenge arrangement close to Highway 50. There is a "Mother Stone" in the middle, with eight surrounding stones marking the four seasons. He named it "Paulhenge."

Paula and Paulhenge: To name a child—or a stone stacking—after oneself: Is it an avenue to unleash your full potential through your offspring and a cairn? Pride?

I, the offspring, and the rock formation may have some things in common. Like the rocks, I am loyal to the Son/Sun. The stacking of stones is an ancient tradition also found in the Old Testament. Paulhenge is a modern cairn that my father Paul constructed beside a busy highway. Jacob of the Bible stacked stones after his dream with a stairway reaching heaven with angels ascending and descending on it. God stood above it and promised Jacob he would not leave him. It was a natural response to mark a place to remind people of God's mighty acts.

The field these stones are arranged in had been tilled by my grandfather and my father. Paul, Paula, and Paulhenge all stand before the Son and declare that his mighty acts are amazing. One in heaven, one on earth, and one using His creation day after day. I don't think it was pride.

"…it is by grace you have been saved."
Grace is a gift. And it is necessary.
I believe my name was a gift. It was necessary.

And I ponder deeply what happens when we are named and when we are forgotten.

I love to wander through antique shops, drifting and dawdling through the vintage tokens, trinkets, and baubles from yesteryear. I like to think about where each item may have come from once upon a time.

A silver pedestal cake plate that served many birthdays.

An iron skillet must have fed a hungry family.

And then I see something that catches my eye: a sepia-toned family photograph in a chipped wooden frame. No date, no names, and no location noted on the front or back. I look closely at the faces. Each person has their own unique expression.

From the attire, it looks like the early 1900s. Women have ankle-length dresses, and men are in suits or button-up shirts with dress pants. The ladies have neat hair, and the guys look like they used an extra dab of hair tonic to get the smart look for the photo.

The portrait is taken on a porch fronted by a yard of dirt and patchy grass. I wonder: is the bleak setting a metaphor for the emotions and outside forces that surround the hearts beating inside the gathered group? The resolute integrity and hopeful encounters of happiness that often characterized this generation—they had stamina and fortitude—could be quelled by class systems, poverty, and tragedy.

Nonetheless, an arched fretwork bracket surrounds the porch entry, encasing the group as if lace were wrapping around them. Does this represent a hedge of protection?

In the front row stands a regal-looking white-haired man, perhaps the patriarch. Next to him is a stately lady with deep-set eyes and dressed in high-laced black boots. White wisps of hair frame her face, and an intricate bun perches atop her head. Is she the matriarch?

No one who passes by this picture will know the names of these souls. As I study the photograph, questions come to mind. What is this stately lady's name? What was the occasion of this day? I would like to ask her, "Who is this man next to you? Is this your home? Did you buy your dress or make it? Who is the small child peeking above the railing? Is there joy in this day?"

Deep down, the reason I am pausing is fear. Fear that I will be forgotten and no one will know my name a few years from now. Decades in the future, a photo will be found in the back of a drawer with everyone wearing coordinating colors. Someone will pick it up and wonder, "Who is this family with matchy-matchy sweaters?" The family that I have raised and made my life mission to embrace and form will be a shadow one hundred years from now. They will be nothing more than faceless names on a genealogy grid. Faces on a Christmas card with signatures. The intricate novelties of our lives will be forgotten. For heaven's sake, I do not know my great-grandparents' lives. Though I knew my great-grandmother, Burton, I did not know her inner life. I do know she didn't like her first name–Pansy. I called her Grandma Burton. Everyone called her Mrs. Burton. If only I had a few moments with her now to ask her about her name.

But even if humans forget our names, God never forgets. Psalm 139:1 says, "You have searched me, LORD, and you know me." We are named and known. God knows all the souls in this antique store photo, just as He knows me right now. He knows where I have come from and where I am going.

In 1998, a seemingly small incident showed me the deep mystery of God's desire to know me. Let me tell you the story.

My paternal grandfather, Albert Morris, was a strong Christian and an active member of the Methodist Church. He and Grandma lived across the field from us. Grandpa Albert died when I was twelve, and things changed after that in many ways. When the patriarch was gone, our lives fell into disrepair like the sparse yard in the antique store photo. The "dirt" became more evident in our yard.

Ten years later, my mom and dad divorced. I was busy with my new married life and career, so although the break-up was difficult and harrowing for my mother, particularly, it didn't affect my immediate existence. Mom and Dad carried on with their own lives. Several years passed, and after my children were born, I developed a greater interest in passing on my faith heritage.

How could I use Grandpa's guidance now? I thought. *I'd like to talk to him about his spiritual journey and life.*

But it was too late; he was gone.

Then, one day, I visited the antique shop my dad and his friend co-owned. I was casually browsing through their antique shop to pass the time. I picked up an old daily prayer book from a stack of books. Each day had a Bible verse and a morning and evening prayer. The price was $1.00.

Great, I thought, *I'll take it.* I turned to the front and read the inscription: "Presented to Albert J. Morris by your Grandfather J. Flick, 1918." My grandfather's name, handwritten by my great-great-grandfather! Grandpa was named and known. Out of the hundreds of books on the shelves, I had touched and opened *this* small black volume, the one with my grandfather's devotionals. This daily prayer book continues to lead my heart as it did for my grandfather all those years ago.

I am named. I am known.

Each of us has a name given by God and given by our parents.

Each of us has a name given by our stature and our smile and given by what we wear.

Each of us has a name given by the mountains and given by our walls.

Each of us has a name given by the stars and given by our neighbors.

Each of us has a name given by our sins and given by our longing.

Each of us has a name given by our enemies and by our love.

Each of us has a name given by our celebrations and given by our work.

Each of us has a name given by the seasons and given by our blindness.

Each of us has a name given by the sea and given by our death.

--Zelda, "Each Man Has a Name", as adapted by Marcia Falk in The Book of Blessings: New York, Harper Collins

1996, p106,ff

Grace in the Desert

My first trip to Arizona:

In the summer of 1974, I was 12, and Mom and Dad took us on a 3-week vacation westward. Driving the northern route to California and the southern route home.

Here, it is a gleaming white Chevrolet truck with a white topper on it. Four bicycles were strapped to the front of the truck, and a twenty-two-foot camper being pulled behind. For most of the over 3500 miles we traveled, my sister (who was 8) and I were in the back of the truck. Yes, in the back of the truck bed with the topper. Conestoga wagon style.

We had a foam mattress that we sat or lay on. We read, talked, and looked out the screened windows. Of course, there was no air conditioning in the back of the truck. The side windows of the topper slid open. There was a window between the truck and toppered back, and we opened it when we wanted to talk to our parents. We loved it. It didn't matter that we were sweating back there, and the muffler and road noise was a gazillion decibels. Never mind the fumes. It was our space. We never questioned our parents about not having a regular car seat to ride in across the country and back. We were going to Mount Rushmore! We were going to California! C'mon—get in the truck and go.

If this had been 40 years later, my parents would have been turned into a government agency. No seat belts, no SEATS --questionable ventilation, and worst offense: no electronic media.

Mount Rushmore, The Tetons, Yellowstone, Washington, Oregon, California, roaring south on the California coastal highway-- we hit San Francisco at rush hour, and the farm family took on the traffic with no GPS. It was exciting looking at the traffic and wondering how Dad was going to maneuver our clomping camper train across the tangled web of cars and bridges. We made it without any trouble using our paper map and stayed outside the city that night.

 Onward, we headed to the desert southwest. Viva Las Vegas. By the time we were there, we were the model for the Chevy Chase family vacation movie. Our camper is dust-laden, and we are ogling over the city that never sleeps. Our hometown had one stoplight, and travelers wave when you pass on the straightaway coming into town. What was this light-laden monstrosity of a city? I was flabbergasted as Dad pulled up to the casinos with our Beverly Hillbilly-style contraption of a rig with no hesitation. I walked into the huge, dark, cavernous gambling buildings with him. One of the security guards told him kids were not supposed to be in the area where we were, but he said something like, "We are just passing through to the bathroom…"

  Dad hustled tickets for two shows: Helen Reddy — fast and loose for our Hoosier family and—the pinnacle of the trip: Tony Orlando and Dawn, "Tie a Yellow Ribbon Round the Old Oak Tree" was the "How Great Thou Art" in my 12-year-old world.

Forgiveness, love, forbearance, and devotion waving in the wind on an oak tree.

Gospel in motion:

"Now the whole damned bus is cheerin'

And I can't believe I see…"

A hundred yellow ribbons round the ole oak tree...

We drove on to the Grand Canyon, across New Mexico, Oklahoma, Texas, and back to Indiana. Arizona–we had to see the Grand Canyon. We stopped to gaze at the beautiful layered bands of rock a mile deep with sweeping vistas and the Colorado River running through it. After about 15 minutes, Dad said, "It's a big hole; we've seen it, let's get on the road."   In 1974, Arizona was a short stop on a long journey.

Arizona today is a long stop. Will it be where I stay? The pilgrimage continues. Tomorrow brings another adventure.

"Yet you do not know what your life will be like tomorrow. You are just a vapor that appears for a little while and then vanishes away." -James 4:14

The Grace of Kindness

✝

What keeps life finely woven together in a cadence? Grace. It never ceases. On the front of my yearly calendar each year, I write: "Jesus is the same yesterday, today, forever." Hebrews 13:8 I use a hard-copy calendar. For me, it is a reliable way to measure time and abide by the moment. I use my sense of touch to turn the paper pages and flip back and forth through the Moleskine book, scanning events and notes throughout the year. It has a handy elastic closure to keep the pages tightly pressed together when it is slipped into a travel case or purse. Even in this technology age, I loyally scrawl on my Moleskine by hand, recording appointments and happenings. My penmanship is neat on some pages and very hurried and messy on others. I write in cursive unless I want it to stand out. Then, I print a word or phrase boldly. My favorite pen is a black fine point.

The words I leave behind will be lost and unremembered. In God's economy, no generation is to be forgotten. Each generation is to be known; their blessings are to be recorded. God values the physical recording of events. Body and Soul. Paper and Pen. Eliminating the physical and focusing on purely spiritual relationships would be dangerous. The calendar and the clock measure time; my physical body records the holy gifts of God's unmerited favor. We are finite beings on earth, bound for eternal life in the new heaven and new earth, yet God values the labor and dust—all that we plow through to get to fertile ground, glory, and grit that we experience in this life.

I walked into my hometown grocery store recently. The woman checking out customers greeted my mother and me—by name. At that moment, memories flooded me. It had been almost thirty years since I had seen her on the Walk to Emmaus. I recalled her embrace, her face, her smile, and how she called me by name all those years before. She was the first person to greet me at a critical point in the weekend. The closing night prayer vigil in which the entire community, having already prayed for each participant in a preceding service, lights candles and sings while the newcomers walk through the glowing group, enjoying the music and reflecting upon the grace and goodness of God. That single moment was important. A millisecond, no words on this paper can describe; however, I believe it was a foretaste of what awaits across the chasm.

"Hello, Gerri," I said, calling her by name. She nodded and smiled. Mom acknowledged her, knowing nothing of the eternal link. Mom pushed the shopping cart toward the aisle.

So much was running through my head. I wanted to embrace Gerri and ask her what she remembered of our brief but awe-inspiring encounter. I halted, considering what to do. Then I knew – the look was enough. Penetrating. Words would not have sufficed. Gerri had called me by name at the right moment; it was enough. It was a taste of the Kingdom, a sacred moment not to be crossed at this time. "I'll talk to her later…For eternity," I thought. I followed Mom.

There are countless ways God's grace and love are experienced in my life daily–some I can see, some I cannot. I hope to continue to notice these moments of grace as I encounter them. The grace is to be counted. The dust and glory are to be counted. I must fall into and over this benevolence infusing my life.

I must record, acknowledge, question, and query the grace of God in my daily moments. Why has he been so gracious to me? I am no more deserving of God's favor than anyone else. The reason he gives me grace is not that I have performed a good work that pleased the Master and merited his mercy. It is of His will and pleasure. He continuously pours what only he can pour over me—Holy Grace—just like he has for people in generations before me.

The sainted Mother Teresa spent her life abiding with Christ in faith, yet she humbly recognized, "I am nothing." In her unwavering humility, she understood that God's grace was *undeserved*. She said, "The more you forget yourself, the more Jesus will think of you." Brother Lawrence wrote, "We cannot escape the dangers which abound in life without the actual and *continual* help of God. Let us, then, pray to Him for it continually." (The Practice of the Presence of God, Ninth Letter) Like Brother Lawrence, I want to "think of Him perpetually" and the abundance of grace with which we can do all things.

The grace poured over yesterday is just as important as the grace poured over today.

And that grace is not limited to this temporary life—it will be in glory. Our lives would be very small indeed if they only consisted of what we experience, touch, and see in the here and now.

We will experience eternal, immeasurable grace amplified.

It is like having your taxes paid forever! Every day is a sunny day. No mosquitoes and sickness.

As Paul writes, "Now we see only a reflection, as in a mirror; then we shall see face to face. Now I know in part; then I will know fully, even as I am fully known." (1 Corinthians 13:12)

The more we glimpse eternity, the more reality and substance our lives will take on. Our existence will be even more real than anything in this visible world.

Thank you, James Tyson, for going before me and acknowledging the grace you encountered.

"All Glory to God."

DEBORAH BY THE PALM • 2014

Made in the USA
Monee, IL
15 February 2024

53208318R00072